"It's time to make a deal."

Taylor continued. "An alliance, a partnership for the purpose of forming a family. Neither one of us can live with a joint-custody arrangement. Still, Justin must have a father and a mother.... So I'm suggesting that we take on the job together."

"Do you mean...." Brooke opened her mouth, but nothing more would come out.

"Yes, this is a prenuptial agreement. I'm asking you to marry me."

"I don't know. I—I guess I always thought I would marry for love."

His gaze was dark, hooded. "Well, isn't that what we would be doing? We both love Justin, don't we?"

FROM HERE TO PATERNITY—romances that feature fantastic men who *eventually* make fabulous fathers. Some seek paternity, some have it thrust upon them, all will make it—whether they like it, or not!

KATHLEEN O'BRIEN, who lives in Florida, started out as a newspaper feature writer, but after marriage and motherhood, she traded that in to work on a novel. She writes with intensity and emotional depth, and we know you'll be gripped by her latest book, *The Daddy Deal*—it will make you laugh, make you cry, and you won't want it to end!

Books by Kathleen O'Brien

Don't miss any of our special offers. Write to us at the following address for information on our newest releases.

Harlequin Reader Service
U.S.: 3010 Walden Ave., P.O. Box 1325, Buffalo, NY 14269
Canadian: P.O. Box 609, Fort Erie, Ont. L2A 5X3

KATHLEEN O'BRIEN

The Daddy Deal

Harlequin Books

TORONTO • NEW YORK • LONDON
AMSTERDAM • PARIS • SYDNEY • HAMBURG
STOCKHOLM • ATHENS • TOKYO • MILAN
MADRID • WARSAW • BUDAPEST • AUCKLAND

To Celie.
Thanks for the wings of your laughter,
the ballast of your wisdom.
And, most of all, for the friendship of a lifetime.

ISBN 0-373-11897-X

THE DADDY DEAL

First North American Publication 1997.

Copyright © 1997 by Kathleen O'Brien.

CHAPTER ONE

TAYLOR PRYCE cursed under his breath as he watched the freckled kid on the swing. Didn't public playgrounds have any supervision? If that kid didn't slow down, he was going to crack his head open like a watermelon.

Hooking his hands through the openings on the chain-link fence, Taylor fought the urge to yell at the boy, who was about five years old and, if he didn't stop trying to turn himself upside down on that swing, probably wouldn't live to be six.

But Taylor managed to control himself. It wasn't his problem. The kid's mother was sitting just ten feet away, placidly gossiping with the other moms. She clearly wasn't worried about how centrifugal force worked, or about concussions and busted skulls. Taylor turned around, unable to bear the gut-twisting suspense of watching the swing lurch higher and higher. It wasn't, he repeated to himself, his problem.

He adjusted the knot on his tie uncomfortably. God, it was going to be a hot day. Checking his watch, he cast a scowling gaze around the park, which was already crowded on this steamy June morning. Kids everywhere. Mothers and infants, fathers and sons, balls and Frisbees and jump ropes. Didn't anyone have to work on a midweek morning anymore? Was everyone in Florida a tourist? And where the devil was McAllister?

The kids on the playground behind him were really turning up the volume, squealing and hollering at one another like wild animals. Again he controlled the urge to turn around and check on the preschool daredevil. It was ridiculous. When had Taylor Pryce, thirty-year-old professional bachelor, developed this sudden fidgety paternal streak?

But, of course, he knew when it had happened—he knew to the day, to the minute. It happened more than a year ago, when he had read an old love letter addressed to his dead brother, a letter that spoke of a baby on the way.

Somehow, ever since that moment, while his lawyers combed the country, searching for that baby, Taylor's subconscious had been training him, getting him ready to be a father.

A father. He shut his eyes against the bright morning sun. God, that sounded strange. Until the letter had surfaced, he hadn't even known he was an uncle. But the letter left no room for doubt. Jimmy, who died two years ago in some crazy, war-torn European country Taylor had hardly known existed, had left behind a child, a little boy, now almost two years old. A boy who should bear the Pryce name—but didn't. A boy who had been... Taylor clenched his teeth. There was only one word for it. Stolen. His nephew had been stolen.

Taylor jerked his tie down an inch and pried his top button loose. It must be a hundred degrees out here. Where the hell was Charlie?

But just as Taylor pulled his keys out of his pocket, ready to head back to his car, Charlie McAllister's pudgy, sweat-drenched face jogged into sight.

"It's about time," Taylor said as Charlie plopped on the bench in front of him, wiping his gleaming face with his terry wristband. "Weren't we supposed to meet at eight?"

Charlie leaned his head back, dramatically out of breath. "Yeah, well, I don't run as fast as I used to." He mopped the sweat from his neck and arms. "And you don't run at all, you lazy son of a gun. How the hell do you stay so fit?"

Taylor just raised his eyebrows—they'd been through this before, and Charlie knew full well that it had something to do with the half-dozen doughnuts he'd scarfed down before his run this morning. Besides, they hadn't met out here to discuss exercise programs. Propping one foot up on the bench beside his friend, Taylor rotated his shoulders slightly, stretching out the tension while he waited for Charlie's heaving chest to slow down.

His patience gave out quickly. Charlie was stalling, and that was a bad sign. "Well?"

Charlie hung his short white towel over his neck and gave Taylor a sorrowful look. "Nothing," he said mournfully. "Zilch."

"Nothing?" Taylor didn't ordinarily waste time repeating the obvious, but he could hardly believe his ears. "Nothing?"

Charlie shrugged. "Well, nothing you can use anyway. Nothing that would seriously impeach her character, or the adoption itself. Apparently, Brooke Davenport adopted Justin in good faith—"

"Good faith?" Taylor leaned over and jammed his forefinger against his thigh angrily. "With my name forged on those adoption papers?"

"We've only your word for that, Taylor." Before Taylor could let loose the oath that rose in his throat, Charlie put up a placating hand. "And don't scowl at me like that. You know what I mean. I'm talking as your lawyer now, and *legally* it's your word against theirs. It's a damned good forgery—even the experts we hired can't agree whether it's a fake."

"It is." Taylor's lips were tight, and the words sounded like a hiss.

"Well, we're going to have to prove that beyond a shadow of a doubt if we expect a judge to take Justin away from the only family he's ever known." Charlie met Taylor's gaze steadily. "Away from what is, by all accounts, a damn good mother."

Taylor narrowed his eyes. "Tell me."

"Okay, but it's really just a bunch of negatives." Charlie took another unnecessary swipe at his upper lip with the towel. "No record, except for a couple of parking tickets. No drugs, no alcohol, no wild nights at the local saloon."

"Boyfriends?"

Charlie shook his head. "Nope. She spends all day with Justin. She works in her garden. Grows a lot of roses. Then at night, she's still working as a nurse, mostly nights, mostly private duty. Not much time for a love life, actually."

"Who's home with Justin all night, then?"

"A nurse friend of hers, older lady."

"What about her?" Taylor knew he was grasping at straws, but damn it, there just had to be some chink in Brooke Davenport's armor. "Any chance this other woman isn't fit...?"

Charlie smiled, obviously following Taylor's line of desperation logic. "You mean is there any chance the old lady is really Ma Barker? Any chance she slips out at night to rob convenience stores, leaving Justin all alone in his crib?" He shook his head. "Sorry. We've already checked her out. She's just a nice, semiretired nurse who rents a room from Brooke in return for a little baby-sitting."

Taylor expelled a frustrated breath and pulled on his left earlobe. "God, Charlie—"

"I know." Charlie's eyes were sympathetic, though his tone was determinedly light. "All the wickedness in this heathen world, and we have to stumble into a nest of saints."

Taylor frowned. Something about all this didn't make sense. "There aren't very many single, twenty-six-year-old female saints around today, Charlie. Why no boyfriends? Is she hideous?"

"Hardly!" Charlie laughed as if the word were a joke, and Taylor wondered just how attractive Brooke Davenport really was. He should have asked to see a picture of her. Though he was considered a tough and astute lawyer, Charlie McAllister was a notorious pushover for a pretty lady, and Taylor had noticed a definite softening in Charlie's attitude toward the whole situation since they had finally located Justin and his adoptive mother.

"So why no men in her life? Surely that's odd in itself."

"No, no." Charlie seemed irritable, as if he resented Taylor's implications. "There've been men, naturally. She was engaged a couple of years ago to a lawyer named Westover. I checked him, too. Good-looking guy, but word is he's a little short on ethics. Anyway, he didn't approve of the adoption, didn't want to be saddled with a damaged kid, I guess, so the relationship went sour."

"Still—"

"And, of course, there was the teenage fiasco—" Charlie stopped himself abruptly, as if he had said something he hadn't meant to say. He fussed with the laces on his jogging shoes. "Anyway, as I said, for our purposes there's nothing. She's normal, but temporarily celibate. She's not a saint, I guess, but she's darn close."

But Taylor wasn't so easily distracted. He straightened slowly. "What teenage fiasco?"

Charlie frowned. "Ancient history," he equivocated, moving to his other shoe, grunting as he bent over farther than his paunch wanted to let him. "Irrelevant."

Taylor frowned, too, glaring down at Charlie's bald spot, which was pink with incipient sunburn. "Whose side are you on here, Charlie?" His voice was hard, even harder than he had intended it to be, and he took a deep breath of muggy air. This thing was really getting to him.

Charlie stopped pretending interest in the shoes. "Yours," he said calmly, meeting Taylor's eyes with the same guileless brown gaze Taylor remembered from childhood, the same straightforward honesty that had made Charlie the undisputed referee of all their crowd's boyhood arguments. "Yours. You know that."

"Then why are you holding back on me? If you've found out something we can use—"

"I haven't." Charlie leaned back with a sigh, wadding his towel up and tossing it roughly onto the bench beside him. "Look, Taylor, I'm telling you it's old news. Ten years old, in fact. When Brooke Davenport was sixteen, she got pregnant. The boyfriend was only a little older— eighteen, I think. Parental apoplexy all around, as you can imagine. Turned out to be an ectopic pregnancy, though, and the poor kid damn near died of it. Lost the baby, of course, and it messed her up so badly there probably won't be any more pregnancies, planned or otherwise."

Taylor could hear the edge that had crept into Charlie's voice, an edge of pity for Brooke Davenport and irritation toward Taylor for pushing the issue. But though he knew it was a sad story, and his heart tightened in spite of himself, Taylor wouldn't allow himself to lose sight of the main point.

"Well, I'm sorry she can't have kids, but that doesn't give her the right to steal someone else's child, does it?"

Charlie's eyes hardened, and suddenly he looked more like the tough opponent other lawyers met in court. "Listen here, Taylor—"

But Taylor ignored the dangerous flash in his friend's eyes. He had a feeling his own eyes looked pretty dangerous right now, too.

"And besides," he went on ruthlessly, "who says we can't use the information? Maybe she's developed an obsession. Maybe being sterile has given her a fixation about adopting, so that she'd do anything to get a baby, even forge my name to those papers. If that could be proved—"

Charlie cursed, an expression of frustration he rarely allowed himself. "God, Taylor, do you hear yourself?"

"What? I'm just being practical. This is no time to get squeamish, Char—"

Before Taylor could finish, a clamor broke out on the playground behind them. Someone was hurt. Above the scuffling of bodies and the confused tumult of voices, Taylor could hear the wailing of a child in pain. He spun around, a foreboding settling in his gut. And he was right—the swing was empty now, twisting crazily back and forth. The freckled little boy was finally on the ground, screaming in fear as his mother knelt next to him, trying to inspect the rapidly reddening scrapes on his cheeks, hands and knees.

Taylor watched the woman fold the kid in her arms, comforting and scolding all at once. Damn! He had known it was going to happen. He should have said something—he should have done something. But he hadn't had the right to get involved. The child wasn't his.

He tried to hold back the sense of impotence that threatened to overwhelm him. Somewhere in this town, his brother's child might be in need, too, and Taylor had no right to get involved in that, either. He cursed under his breath. It was unendurable.

He wheeled back toward Charlie. "I'm going to get him," he said, his voice sounding as if it had been scoured with sandpaper. "I don't care what you think. I don't care what anybody thinks. That boy is my nephew. My flesh and blood. And, by God, I'm going to take him back from that woman if it's the last thing I do."

To his surprise, Charlie's gaze was once again sympathetic, drifting from the scene on the playground to Taylor, then back to the crying boy again. Finally, he nodded. "Okay," he said. "We'll think of something."

"I already have," Taylor said curtly, pulling his pen out of the breast pocket of his jacket. "Give me the woman's address."

Charlie recoiled subtly, his eyes narrowing. "Why? I thought you didn't want me to approach her. I thought you didn't want me to let her know we were investigating."

"I don't." Taylor held out the pen and a slim black notebook, pointing them at Charlie's chest like weapons. "Just give me her address."

The lawyer took the pen reluctantly. "What the devil are you planning?" He began, very slowly, to write, and Taylor waited silently while he scribbled a few words on the page.

Sighing deeply, he handed the notebook to Taylor, who gave it only one short glance before flipping it shut. One glance was all he needed. 909 Parker Lane—he'd remember that address until the day he died.

Turning his head away from Charlie's disapproving frown, Taylor watched the little boy hobble off the playground, sobbing inconsolably into his mother's skirt. He could feel Charlie standing behind him, his anxiety and annoyance almost as palpable as the heat around them.

"I asked you a question," Charlie said slowly. "What are you planning to do?"

Taylor turned his head an inch. He could just see the other man out of the corner of his eye.

"Whatever it takes," he said grimly, sliding the notebook back into his breast pocket. "Whatever it takes."

Was it just that she was so tired, Brooke Davenport wondered, or was the Eberson Theater looking particularly surreal tonight?

Ordinarily, Brooke loved the exotic old movie palace, which dated from the Roaring Twenties. The auditorium walls were covered with sculpted facades to suggest an open-air Mediterranean courtyard; its ceiling was painted violet, like a twilight sky, and dotted with electric "stars".

Tonight, though, as she followed Clarke Westover through the glittering throng of wealthy Floridians who had gathered to raise money for the theater's ongoing restoration, Brooke suddenly found the atmosphere unnerving. She swept her tired gaze across the walls that climbed up toward the artificial twilight. Not one square inch had been left uncarved. Scrolls, vines, flowers, birds and cherubs all twisted together in nightmarish intimacies. It was almost suffocating.

Or perhaps the auditorium was just too crowded. She took a deep breath of the stuffy, overconditioned air and tried to ignore the champagne that splashed over her knuckles as yet another tuxedo bumped into her. The seats had been removed—the latest phase of the renovation—and replaced for the evening with a temporary floor and small wrought-iron tables and chairs. Brooke looked longingly at every empty chair they passed. She was so tired—she had barely slept for the past week. If only Clarke had agreed to meet her in his office. This whole ordeal could have been over by now.

Instead, it was just beginning. Climbing to the stage, the emcee tapped his microphone and announced that it was time to open the auction. An expectant murmur rode through the room like a wave, and the guests began gliding toward their seats, a psychedelic rainbow of silk swirling against a checkerboard of black-and-white tuxedos.

Brooke was just barely able to keep up with Clarke's broad, black-clad back—he was moving fast, more accustomed than she to maneuvering through elegant party crushes. Without warning, the room dimmed as someone turned down the stars, and for a frightening second Brooke wondered if she were fainting.

"Clarke..."

She clutched at his hand for balance, a moment of weakness she regretted when she saw his surprised smile broaden into self-satisfaction. Ahhh, that smile said— now he had her precisely where he wanted her. After almost two years of keeping a strained distance, she had finally come crawling back to him, just as he had always predicted she would.

Except that it wasn't true. When she had telephoned him this morning, she'd been scrupulously careful to explain that her call was strictly business. But she had known, from the minute he insisted on meeting her at this society function, that he was reading something more personal into it.

What a mess! She tried to extricate her hand unobtrusively, but his cold grip was proprietary and unyielding. Finally, just as she began to feel slightly claustrophobic, Clarke found the table assigned to them and pulled out her chair with a flourish.

She sat, her whole body sinking with relief, though the iron was stiff and unwelcoming. When Clarke draped his arm loosely around the back of her chair, Brooke pretended not to notice. She knew she had to tread very carefully. If she wounded his pride, he would find a way to make her pay.

Exhausted tears suddenly stung behind Brooke's eyes. How high would the price be? Would he refuse to help her, to talk to Mr. Alston for her? Or would he go even further? He knew that Alston, the millionaire builder whose legal affairs he handled, was the one man in Tampa who actually desired Brooke's little bungalow enough to pay three times its appraised value. Could Clarke possibly be capable of advising Mr. Alston *not* to buy?

"Seven hundred once, twice—" The gavel thumped, echoing in the microphone, and Brooke started slightly. "Sold to Mr. Westover, number twenty-three, for seven hundred dollars."

She looked up, stunned. She hadn't even realized that Clarke was bidding on anything, hadn't, in truth, even realized the auction was under way. Seven hundred dollars? Good Lord, what was he buying? She glanced over at him, and even in the dim light she could see the flush of triumph on his features.

"Bastard thought he was going to take it away from me," Clarke muttered to her out of the side of his mouth.

"Who?" She was confused, as if he were speaking a foreign language. "Take what away?"

"Number three-oh-four." Clarke shifted his eyes subtly to the table on their immediate right, where a man sat, absently tapping his card on the arm of his chair while he chatted softly with a stunning brunette. "See him? Taylor Allen. Man's a damn fool. It's a good case of champagne, but not that good. It's not worth more than six hundred."

Brooke wasn't sure which of the two men had been proved the bigger fool—Taylor What's-his-name, who had lost the opportunity to overpay for the case of champagne, or Clarke, who seemed so smugly pleased to have done so—but she knew better than to voice any such thoughts. Clarke had caught Taylor's eye, and the other man raised his glass with a small smile, as if saluting Clarke's acumen. Clarke returned the gesture, bowing slightly, and Brooke inwardly flinched. Was she the only one who saw the mockery in Taylor's eyes?

"Usher!" Clarke's sudden whisper, spoken over his shoulder, was sharp and piercing. "We'll have a bottle now." The usher nodded and disappeared, and Clarke turned to Brooke. "To celebrate," he said softly. "An important champagne for an important night."

"Clarke..." She leaned forward, suddenly desperate to straighten things out now, before they went too far. "Clarke, I hope you understand that I just wanted to ask you—"

"Shhh..." The emcee had begun hawking a celebrity autograph. Clarke had returned his attention to the stage, though she could tell he was watching Taylor out of the corner of his eye, waiting to see whether the other man desired the item before he bid on it.

Clarke needn't have bothered. Taylor couldn't have been more disinterested. His brunette, whose preferred method of communication seemed to be through her fingertips, was talking to him, and their heads were bent together in a heart-shaped shadow. Brooke watched them for a moment, envying the brunette her utter sangfroid.

The woman was quite beautiful, and judging from the understated glamour of her dress, she had no money problems, no sick child at home. No, the brunette had nothing more troubling on her mind than whether she could make Taylor kiss her.

Even that didn't seem to be much in question. As Brooke watched, too tired to subdue the demon of envy, the man smiled at some soft coquetry the brunette tossed his way. And what a smile... For a space no longer than the pulse of a heartbeat, something intensely female lurched inside Brooke, something warm and electric she hadn't felt in years—something she certainly hadn't expected to feel tonight.

The sensation disappeared as quickly as it came, though. Feeling foolish, Brooke averted her eyes and gulped down some of Clarke's seven-hundred-dollar champagne, which the obedient usher had just poured into her glass.

She drank again, aware of growing slightly tipsy, blessedly numb. How depressing. How desperately depressing. It was proof of how exhausted she really was that, even after a glimpse of that smile, she still wanted more than anything to go home and sleep—alone—for a week.

Was she really a dried-up old woman at only twenty-six? Had the past two years of constant worry—worry about expensive doctors and painful operations and her little boy sobbing in bewildered pain—left her with a heart too withered to enjoy, even for a moment, a handsome man's beautiful, sexy smile?

Finally, halfway through the second bottle, the auction was over. Though by now she could hardly feel her tongue, could hardly string her words together with anything approaching eloquence or diplomacy, she began trying to explain to Clarke why she had asked to see him.

She heard it all as if someone else were speaking.

"The doctors say Justin's new skin graft has to be done right away," she said. "They think the old one, the one just above his rib cage, has healed awkwardly— and it might be restricting the use of his left arm." She was proud of the matter-of-fact tone she achieved. The words might be slurred a little, but at least they weren't spoken through tears. "So I have to find more money, and I have to find it soon."

Clarke's face seemed colder than before, more remote. "What about your inheritance from your grandmother? You told me you'd use that to finance Justin's medical care."

"It's gone." In her mind's eye, Brooke could see the rapidly decreasing numbers marching across her bank statements. The inheritance had been small to begin with. Two years of expensive surgeries had been like an open drain, and the money had flowed through it in a flood. "I . . ." She tried to think of a way to put it. "I guess I underestimated the number of op—"

Clarke broke in with a bitter laugh. "I told you, didn't I? I knew you had no idea what you were getting into. No idea at all."

"No," she agreed meekly. He was right. She hadn't listened to him, hadn't even wanted to know. You couldn't put a price tag on love. She had been rescuing Justin, an orphan in a dangerous foreign country, from being sold to the highest bidder by two uncles who had no interest in taking responsibility for a badly burned, badly frightened infant. What did it matter, in such a case, how much the doctors were going to cost?

"You were right. I had no idea at all." She leaned forward. "Anyway, the bungalow is the only asset I have left."

Clarke raised his brows. "It's pretty small. Is it worth enough to pay for the operation?"

"No." She bit her lower lip and folded her hands, white-knuckled, on the table in front of her. "That's why I needed to see you. Your Richard Alston has always wanted to buy it, you know. A few years ago he offered me almost three times its appraised value."

Clarke nodded warily. "Yes, but you turned him down. As I recall, he told you then he'd never make the offer again. He's not a man who takes rejection well. He's not accustomed to it."

She drew in a deep breath and tried to sound sweet— the way Clarke liked her. "I know. That's why I'm coming to you. I was hoping you might be able to coax him into reinstating the offer. Maybe not at the full price he offered before, but something—something that would help me cover the expenses . . ."

Halfway through the speech, she saw Clarke's face was tightening. His lips seemed to be closing in on themselves, his eyes disappearing into the folds of their lids.

He was furious. Oh, God. She had so hoped that he could put their personal issues behind him long enough to see that the suggestion she was making him could benefit *both* of them. But the sight of his tense, offended features was far from reassuring, and she swallowed hard before finishing up in a rush of awkward words.

"So I was hoping that perhaps you could set something up." She smiled ingratiatingly. "It could work to your advantage, too, earn you some goodwill if he realizes you're the one making it possible. He might be grateful, and—''

"Wait a minute." Clarke broke through Brooke's stumbling explanations, waving his right hand, his diamond-studded signet ring glinting under the electric stars. "Are you telling me that all of this—your call, our date—this really *is* just about business?"

His color had risen along with his voice, and Brooke had to steel herself not to flinch. All around them, people who had been murmuring politely over their champagne glasses were casting curious, sidelong glances their way.

His scowl, though fierce, looked suddenly a lot like the approach of one of Justin's two-year-old tantrums, and even through her anxiety, Brooke felt a surge of relief that she hadn't actually married this man. She must have been mad, quite completely mad, ever to have considered it.

"I did say it was just business." She defended herself mildly, trying not to inflame him any further, but her tone was firm. "I wanted to meet at your office, but you insisted on bringing me here—"

"I didn't have *time* at my office." Clarke's flush deepened. "You said it had to be today, and I was booked solid. I'm a damned busy man, Brooke."

"I know you are." She forced herself to soothe him. "I'm grateful, really I am, that you're making the time to talk to me now. And of course I'm pleased to get the chance to be part of such a lovely evening...."

She rattled on, not allowing herself to feel humiliated by hand-feeding this petty man's ego. It was for Justin, she reminded herself desperately.

She gave it her best, but Clarke was clearly only marginally mollified. Finishing his drink with a sharp, backward toss of his head, he drummed his fingers on the small wrought-iron table between them and let his eyes roam the room, checking out the other guests, refusing to meet Brooke's gaze.

"So what do you think?" She was losing patience with his petulance. Though she knew it was suicidal, the champagne was playing havoc with her self-control. "Do you think Mr. Alston is still interested? I really need to sell the house soon, Clarke."

Clarke swiveled in his chair. "Jennifer!" he cried in patently feigned surprise. "Look, there's Jennifer Hanlon!" He stood, excusing himself curtly with a wave of his hand and, with a deliberate discourtesy, pushed his way through the crush of bodies toward a lovely blonde swathed in mink.

At first, Brooke was too stunned to be angry. Her gaze followed him numbly, watching his slow, self-important progress through the crowd. The dancing was just about to begin, the orchestra already in the pit, tuning up, and the floor was dense with people, all of whom seemed to know Clarke. He stopped every few feet, eager to slap another back, shake another hand.

She tilted her head down, trying to compose herself. What a fool she had been to think that Clarke would help her. He didn't understand anything. He still thought life was just a power play, where you lived for the chance to one-up your enemies.

He didn't have any idea how far she had traveled beyond that pinched world of his. He had no idea what it was like to be a parent, to love someone more than you loved yourself. And he didn't know real grief—didn't know what it felt like to hear your child crying, begging you to make his pain go away, every syllable falling onto your raw nerves like the lash of a whip, maddening you, making you choke on your own impotent rage and fear, making you offer fate any Faustian bargain you can imagine.

But fate was deaf and didn't answer.

She drew a deep breath, squeezing her eyes shut. Maybe she should call home. It was only nine, and maybe Justin hadn't fallen asleep yet. Gretchen let him stay up late, and Brooke couldn't really blame her for it. When he begged for one more story, it was terribly hard to say no. They were spoiling him, Brooke knew. But he had been through so much....

Yes. She'd call home. She dug blindly through her purse. Hearing Justin's voice would chase these stupid tears back where they belonged. Justin was her focus. She would just call to say good-night one more time—

"Are you all right?"

At the sound of a strange masculine voice, Brooke looked up guiltily, her hands frozen knuckle-deep in her purse as if she had been caught burrowing through someone else's wallet instead of her own. To her shock, the man who had battled Clarke over the case of champagne—Clarke had said his name was Taylor, Taylor something, what was his last name?—was standing next to her. Alone. His brunette had vanished.

A stray tear dribbled onto the corner of her mouth, and Brooke felt herself flushing. He was watching her quietly, studying her with the dispassionate curiosity he might have given an intriguing but perplexing painting. She knew what he was thinking. He was probably wondering why she sat here alone downing champagne in the wake of a date who was conspicuously ignoring her. Wondering why she was pale and on the verge of a crying jag. Wondering, perhaps, whether that meant she was an easy mark...

She tried to lick the tear from her lip unobtrusively. Strange. He didn't look like the kind of man who had to prey on other men's rejects. In this dim light, some of the details were unclear—eye color, for instance—but he projected the confidence of a man accustomed to finding a welcome wherever he went. Now that he had unfolded himself from the chair, she saw that he was at least six foot two. He wore that tuxedo as if he'd been born in it.

And that smile...

He was holding out a snowy, softly folded handkerchief, smiling at her over his outstretched hand. It was a slow smile, and when it reached his eyes it lit them from within, revealing green sparks that were at once strangely new and amazingly familiar.

"Thank you." She forced herself to smile back as she accepted the handkerchief. His expression was calmly neutral, but somehow it seemed to impart strength to her. "To tell you the truth, though," she said, blotting her eyes carefully, then returning the slightly soggy white square with an apologetic grimace, "I was actually digging around in here looking for a quarter."

He tilted his head, silently speculating, but without a word he extracted a silver coin from his pocket and held it out.

Brooke's face burned—she must have sounded as if she were panhandling the man—but there was nothing to do but take the quarter. "Thank you," she said again stiffly, closing her hand around it, feeling its hard, cool edges grow warm in her palm.

"The pay phones are in the lobby," he said conversationally, as if he handed money to crying ladies every day. "But I'm sure one of the ushers will call a taxi for you if you need a ride home."

"A taxi?" She was momentarily confused, but she followed his gaze across the room and saw that he was looking at Clarke, who was still clutching the blonde, his fingers buried deep in the mink that caressed her shoulders. "Oh..." She shook her head. "No, I just need to call home to check on my son. I'm not leaving."

"Really?" He raised one brow. "Why not?"

Such unexpected bluntness confused her, and she stared stupidly for a moment, as if she hadn't understood him. "Why not?" she echoed hollowly. Oh, God, why had she drunk so many glasses of champagne? She must sound like an idiot. "Well, because Clarke is coming right back. We were in the middle of a rather important discussion, you see, so he'll have to come right back...."

But even as she spoke, she saw that Clarke was now at the far side of the auditorium, his cellular telephone held self-importantly to his ear, and the blonde still clinging to his arm. He stopped for a moment at the door, saying something to the usher without even lowering the flip phone.

The usher nodded uncertainly, looking uncomfortable, but Clarke spoke sharply to the younger man, who nodded again and began picking his way hurriedly back toward Brooke's table. She watched his approach helplessly, a dread certainty settling like a weight in her chest.

"Mr. Westover says he regrets he's been called away," the usher said when he finally made it across the room. He looked a bit confused himself. "An emergency. He asked me to tell you."

Brooke nodded. Fury and humiliation warred within her, and the result was a strange, passive paralysis. "Thanks," she said, as if he had brought her a present. And then, nonsensically, again. "Yes, well. Thank you."

"Ummm..." The young man shifted from one foot to the other and bit his lip. "Um, the thing is, someone needs to settle Mr. Westover's bill."

Brooke slowly turned and stared at the young man blankly. "His bill?" The word had no meaning, really. It was just a collection of sounds. How could Clarke have left her here? If she had imagined a hundred cruel paybacks, she could never have thought of this one. She didn't know another soul in this room. Struggling single-mom nurses didn't exactly hobnob with Tampa's social royalty.

"Well, yes, you see...Mr. Westover bought some champagne at the auction, remember?" He looked pointedly at the glass she held in her trembling hand. "You're drinking it now. But no one paid for it, you see, and now Mr. Westover seems to have left, and well, I wondered if maybe he had left his credit card with you...."

Brooke whirled, horrified. She set her champagne glass on the table as if it had been poisoned. Seven hundred dollars? Was Clarke insane? Where on earth was she going to get seven hundred dollars? Just five minutes ago she would have considered herself wealthy if she'd been able to dredge up a quarter. She dropped onto the chair, trying to make the suddenly tilting room stand still.

Brooke was hardly a socialite, but even she understood that people who bid at fund-raisers were as honor bound as poker players to make good their debts. She half expected someone to call the manager, to call the police, to tie an apron around her blatantly inferior party dress and send her in to wash the dishes.

Suddenly, she felt an overwhelming, irrational urge to laugh. Seven hundred dollars was a whole lot of dishes.

"No, no, he didn't give me any instructions," she managed to say. Somehow she forced herself to look at the man beside her, who had been a nonchalant spectator through the whole embarrassing scene. To her shock, he was smiling composedly down at the perspiring usher. And he was holding out a silver credit card between two long, perfectly shaped fingers.

"It's no problem at all," he was saying soothingly. "I'm sure it was just an oversight on Mr. Westover's part. I'll get him to reimburse me tomorrow."

"Oh, no!" She couldn't let this happen. Brooke reached up and clutched the man's arm. "No, you mustn't!"

But it was too late. The usher, not fool enough to let such a simple solution slip through his fingers, had already whisked the credit card out of the man's dark hand. She stared at him, sinking back against the stiff iron of her chair.

"Mr...." she began miserably, wishing she at least could remember his name.

He smiled. "Call me Taylor," he said graciously.

"Taylor," she repeated weakly. "You mustn't do that. It's not up to you to—"

"But I already did." He pulled out the chair that Clarke had vacated and, settling himself comfortably in it, turned his beautiful smile toward Brooke.

"But you can't be sure that Clarke will—"

"It doesn't matter." He held up the half-empty bottle that still perched in its nest of ice. "I was bidding on it anyway. I'll be perfectly happy to own the case myself, if it comes to that. It will be reward enough if you'll invite me to share a glass with you. I think I'd like to make a toast."

She frowned. She must have had too much champagne. She couldn't catch up somehow, couldn't follow the dizzying turn of events. Catch up? Good heavens— when he smiled at her like that, she couldn't even catch her breath.

"A toast?"

"Yes," he said, pouring each of them half a glass, then lifting his. "To Clarke Westover, wherever he is right now."

Her frown deepened. "Do you know Clarke?"

He nodded. "Oh, yes. I know him." His voice had undertones she couldn't decipher, but he didn't give her time to dwell on them. "Let's toast him, then, for being such a busy man. For leaving this chair empty." He grinned disarmingly. "You see, I've been wanting to meet you all night."

She knew her cheeks pinkened at the compliment, which pleased her inordinately. He was a very handsome man after all, and the room was ripe with beautiful women. The wriggle of sensual warmth, that delicious female awareness she had felt when she first saw this man, had returned. In spite of the awkward circumstances, she felt strangely exhilarated, triumphant, as if she had proved something. Proved, perhaps, that she wasn't quite an old, dried-up woman yet.

After all, it wasn't quite so terrible, not if he really knew Clarke. Clarke would reimburse him tomorrow, as Taylor had said. Still, a dim note of caution sounded. Something in all this didn't make sense.

"But if you know Clarke," she said, trying to verbalize that hazy uncertainty, "then why didn't you come over when he was still here?"

He smiled again, and in that moment she almost felt as if he were an old, trusted friend. His eyes were so familiar somehow, so warm and full of intelligence, full of sympathy. And yet she knew she'd never met him before. If she had, she never could have forgotten it.

Already, though, her nerves were relaxing, and she picked up her glass slowly. Logic be damned. She liked this man, whoever he was. She liked him very much. Now if only he could answer the question, could still her suspicions, and let her give in to the pleasurable glow that was stealing through her.

"If you know Clarke," she repeated, "why didn't you join us when he was here?"

"That should be obvious, I'd think," he answered, clinking the rim of his glass against hers. "Because I simply cannot stand the man."

CHAPTER TWO

AT FIRST, she was speechless. He'd uttered the words casually, in the offhand way he might have expressed a dislike for broccoli, and she wasn't at all sure how she should respond. Stalling, she brought her glass to her lips and drank, studying him over the rim, looking for a cue.

To her surprise, his green eyes were alight with an irreverent sparkle. It was infectious, and in spite of herself she felt a smile tickling at her lips. As she began to grin, she felt something odd happening inside her. It was as if a logjam of oppression burst loose with an almost audible pop, and she was washed by a sudden, delicious sensation of freedom.

"Now that you mention it," she said, still grinning, "I can't stand Clarke, either."

"Oh?" He raised one brow.

Nodding, she took another sip, wondering whether this last glass might have pushed her judgment over the edge. Perhaps instead of being forthright and bold, she was merely being drunk. But did it really make any difference? She felt freer than she had in months. She felt good.

"Absolutely cannot *stand* him. So that makes two of us. Good thing we didn't marry him, isn't it?"

"Very." The creases at the corner of his eyes grew more pronounced. "I for one am deeply relieved."

"Me, too." She stared into her champagne, then sipped again thoughtfully. "The bottom line," she confided, "is that Mr. Clarke Westover is an assous pomp."

But that hadn't come out quite right. "A passous..." She frowned and gave up. "A jerk."

She punctuated her pronouncement by swigging an emphatic mouthful of bubbles, but just as she did so, she glimpsed the smile quirking Taylor's lips. Immediately, a dangerous spasm of answering laughter tightened her chest. She swallowed quickly and lowered her glass, trying not to spill the champagne as she began to giggle. But the table was small, and her aim was faulty. She knocked her glass against the edge of his, and the stem rocked dangerously. It finally righted itself, but not before spraying a fine mist of liquid across the outer edge of her hand and onto the tabletop.

"Hey," he said, leaning over to dab the moisture from her knuckles with the handkerchief he had once again magically produced. "Careful. We're never going to get our money's worth out of this champagne if you keep flinging it around like that."

Our money's worth. She noticed how instinctively thoughtful he was, how even his pronouns were chosen to minimize her self-consciousness. His touch was very deft, almost impersonal—it held no hint of sleazy opportunism. Over his ministering hand, they smiled at each other in a companionable harmony.

She knew she should feel like a fool. And yet somehow she wasn't at all embarrassed. He had a gift for making people comfortable, she realized, though perhaps it was merely a lucky by-product of his own sublime self-confidence.

"I'm sorry," she said sheepishly, shoving her glass to one side. "A friend of mine once had a great word for this. Spiff—" she struggled to get her lips around the syllables correctly "—spifflicated." She smiled. "I'm afraid I'm getting spifflicated."

"No, you're not." He picked up her hand and swabbed champagne efficiently from the underside. "In fact, in some counties they use that as a legal test. If you can actually pronounce 'spifflicated', you're not.''

"Still," she said, eying the last two inches of golden bubbles in her glass and shuddering. "That's it for me."

She knew, even as she said it, that he might interpret her words as the excuse he needed to get up and say goodbye. His chivalrous mission was accomplished—he had rescued her from Clarke's petty cruelties. He had loaned her a quarter, paid the astronomical auction bill and wiped her fingers. He had even salvaged her pride— letting everyone in the room see that, though Clarke had abandoned her, she was not entirely friendless. Best of all, he had made her laugh.

It was more unselfish generosity than she had ever received from anyone, much less from a total stranger. She had no right to expect more. Or even to wish for it. She had to let him leave now, if he wanted to.

But he made no move to stand. Instead, he poured himself another glass of champagne and leaned back, stretching his shoulders against the iron rim of the chair, getting comfortable. Her hopes shot up like a kite in a gusting wind, and she suddenly realized how much, how very much, she had hoped he would stay.

"You were with someone earlier," she began hesitantly, strangely reluctant to broach the subject, but knowing she had to. There was no point in letting herself dream if that slinky brunette was going to return from the ladies' room any minute and reclaim her white knight. "Is she still here?"

"No," he said, meeting her gaze directly, without a trace of self-consciousness. "She wasn't my date. I met her only a couple of hours ago. In fact, I don't really know most of the people here. I don't live in Florida. I'm from Massachusetts, from a little town in the Berkshires."

Not from Tampa, then—not even a Floridian. She couldn't have been more surprised. He had certainly looked right at home with this crowd. She supposed that being very, very rich was like belonging to an exclusive fraternity—no matter where you traveled, you could always look up the local chapter and be assured of fitting right in.

Still, she knew the tickets to this fund-raiser had been exorbitant. Surely there were places back home in the Berkshires with more legitimate claim on his charity.

"So why are you here?" She waved her hand toward the stage. Then she worried—had that sounded rude? She seemed to have dropped her tact down the bottom of that last champagne bottle. "I mean, this is just a little local theater. Why would you come here...?"

He narrowed his eyes thoughtfully and took another slow swallow of champagne. He held her gaze so long she began to wish she hadn't asked. Perhaps he thought she was overstepping the bounds of their extremely short acquaintance. He couldn't understand, couldn't even know, that she felt strangely as if she'd known him a long, long time. She couldn't even really understand it herself.

Finally he smiled. "If I said I came here to see you, you probably wouldn't believe it, would you?"

She grinned and shook her head. "I think that line only works after *three* bottles."

"I was afraid of that." He spread his hands, palms up, surrendering the notion. "Actually, I'm in Tampa because—" he paused "—because I have family here."

"Not a wife, though?" She could hardly believe her audacity. But it seemed, in her champagne logic, to be better dealt with now than later.

He shook his head. "Not a wife."

"Or a girlfriend?"

He shook his head again, and a reluctant smile crooked his mouth appealingly. "Not even female."

"Good." She relaxed as if she had settled a question of major philosophical importance. "Then you don't have to leave."

"No. I'm free to indulge my own pleasure tonight." He picked up his glass and swirled the liquid in it, as if admiring the way the bubbles burst golden under the electric starlight. "And it would please me very much to spend the evening with you." He glanced up. "Assuming, of course, that you're equally free."

She waved her hand toward the exit through which Clarke had so recently slipped. "Well, as you can see, I have no date—"

"And no one waiting at home, wondering where you are?"

She shook her head. "The only male at my house is two years old, and he'd better not be wondering anything. He'd better be sound asleep." She raised her chin slightly. "Justin is my son."

This, too, seemed like something she needed to make clear from the outset. A lot of men remembered they had urgent appointments elsewhere the minute they learned she had a child. She watched Taylor's handsome face carefully, looking for the familiar signs of shock, disappointment or disapproval. A son, but no husband...

His expression was hard to read. He didn't look threatened, and he certainly didn't exhibit any moral indignation. But he did look intensely interested, thoughtful, somehow, as if he were trying to assemble a picture that wouldn't quite come together for him. That was all right, she decided. A little mystery did more to enhance a woman's appeal than a boatload of diamonds. And she did want to appeal to him. She wanted it with a raw intensity that was growing stronger by the minute.

"Tell me," he said finally, his green eyes quizzical, "when you said you were glad you hadn't married

Westover, was that just an academic observation? Or had you really considered it?''

"Considered it?" She shook her head again, as if she could hardly believe the truth herself. "I was his fiancée for almost two years." Looking down at her now-unadorned left hand, she sighed. "Of course, I was out of the country for one of those years, so it's only half as stupid as it sounds."

"Why?"

"I don't know, really. I've asked myself that a hundred times." She gazed toward the door, where she had last seen Clarke. "I guess it's because, though you'd never know it from tonight's performance, he can charm the petals off a rose when he wants to. And because I was lonely—"

She stopped, something in his expression suddenly warning her that she was answering the wrong question. She flushed. "Oh...you mean why was I out of the country for a year?"

He nodded. "You have to admit it's...different. Your average, hot-blooded American woman, upon becoming engaged, doesn't just grab her passport and emigrate."

"Well, I was already committed to going overseas before Clarke asked me to marry him," she explained rather heatedly, as if he had accused her of possessing a tepid nature. Of being passionless. "People were counting on me. I'm a nurse, and I was part of a volunteer medical team our hospital sponsored. The country we were sent to was being torn apart by civil war."

She leaned forward, squeezing her hands together, trying to make him feel the urgency of her obligation. It wasn't fair for him to judge her. She wasn't a cold woman, though Clarke had used that argument against her frequently. She *wasn't*. "People were dying."

"Well, then, of course you had to go," he said, running his fingers lightly over her whitened knuckles, his smile reassuring. "And if Clarke Westover had been half a man, he would have packed up his fax machine and gone with you."

She tried to smile back, but foolish tears were pooling along her bottom lids, and she had to look away, afraid that he would see them. She wasn't sure why she suddenly felt like crying. Perhaps the memories of that desperate, blood-soaked year were too close. Or perhaps it was because no one had looked at her like that in a long time, with sympathy and understanding and...amazingly, there was admiration, too.... No, not in a very long time.

Or maybe it was just the champagne. *Get a grip*, she told herself. If you turn into one of those dismal, weepy drunks, this white knight of yours will disappear faster than you can say spifflicated.

"What's wrong?" Taylor's hand settled over hers, cupping her tense fingers in his cool, soothing palm. "Is it about Clarke?"

"No. No, I'm glad he's gone." Without looking at him, she shook her head. She didn't trust herself to try to explain. She had forgotten how drinking lowered her defenses—or perhaps she had just forgotten how completely she had begun to rely on those defenses to get her through.

"Then what is it?" His voice was low and warm. She could just barely hear it over the sound of violins as the conductor waved the orchestra into a plaintive version of "For All We Know". "Tell me."

Again she shook her head, appalled at how tempting it was to think about giving in, breaking down, handing her too-heavy heart to this man who seemed so strong, so thoroughly capable of taking care of it. She felt him stroking the back of her hand, his fingers sensitive and sure, and she had to bite her lips together, for fear the words would come tumbling out—private, mortifying

little words that could only shame her. Words like lonely.
Empty. Frightened.

"Nothing," she said tightly. "It's nothing."

For a moment he was silent. And then she sensed him
rising.

"Come with me," he said, holding out his hand.

She finally looked up slowly, from the lean, ridged
pads of his palm up to where the golden-tanned skin of
his wrist disappeared into the snowy cuff of his dress
shirt. "Where?"

"We're going to dance," he said, curving his fingers
to beckon her toward him. "I think they're playing our
song."

At first, she didn't move. She looked up the long
creases of the black tuxedo sleeve, up to where he towered
over her. And she realized, with a sudden shivering heat
at the base of her spine, that she found Taylor so attractive it terrified her. She hadn't thought about men
that way in a long, long time. Not even Clarke—although
she had certainly tried to. When Clarke had kissed her,
she'd found it difficult to keep her mind off other things,
like the laundry or how she was going to pay the electricity bill next month. Ironic, wasn't it? Her fiancé's
kisses had left her completely unmoved, yet the thought
of dancing with this stranger made her knees go hopelessly warm and mushy.

She couldn't stop studying him, though she wondered
if she was taking too long to answer. She suspected that,
in her muzzy mental state, time had begun to lose its
firm contours like an overused rubber band.

What was it about him that melted her from the inside
out? Oh, he was gorgeous. No question about that, even
though she supposed that, strictly speaking, his nose was
too strong, rising too arrogantly from high between his
brows. But the strong lines of those dark brows were so
perfectly aligned with his dramatic cheekbones and

sculpted jaw that the effect was both beautiful and noble, as if he were an illustration in some elegant magazine.

But she had known plenty of handsome men. Perhaps, she thought, her gaze drifting down, it was that strange sense of familiarity in his green-flecked eyes. That haunting sense of déjà vu...

"You know," Taylor said mildly, glancing pointedly at his still-outstretched hand, "I'm beginning to look like a fool."

Blushing, Brooke rose quickly. Too quickly. Her blood swooped to her feet, leaving her head empty and dizzy. She swayed toward him, and he caught her in one strong arm.

"That's better," he said, his lips close to her ear. Putting his arm around her shoulder, he tucked her up against him and led her to the stage, where dozens of couples were already jammed together. There didn't seem to be a free inch, but somehow Taylor found a niche near the edge of the proscenium arch, where a statue of Neptune, backlit with an eerie violet glow, stared at them through blind white eyes.

Taylor slid his arm around her waist, pulling her in to face him, and for several minutes they shifted slowly to the music, each holding away from the other a bit stiffly, as if neither wanted to be the first to make a move toward a deeper intimacy. But the poignant song was wrapping itself around them, and before she knew it her hand was nestled between his fingers and his heart, and her head had dropped against the cool black lapel of his tuxedo.

The song ended, but they didn't move, waiting until the violinists' bows began the dip and thrust of another love song. As the wistful strains of "Lara's Theme" from *Dr. Zhivago* filled the air, Taylor's hand tightened on the small of her back, massaging softly, nudging her into motion.

After that, Brooke didn't even try to fight the slow fusion that brought their bodies ever closer together— her cheek rubbing against his shoulder, her breast brushing his chest, and their thighs braiding rhythmically, together, then apart. Shutting her eyes, she breathed deeply, learning the crisp, lime-fresh scent of him that rose subtly under her nostrils, stirred by her touch—a scent that was both reassuringly wholesome and surprisingly sexual.

He was far more intoxicating than champagne, Brooke thought dreamily, and she felt something flickering to life inside her, like a small, buried flame suddenly brought into the air. She turned her focus inward, visualizing the flame—once a pale and helplessly guttering flutter—as it grew into a steady, red-hot tongue of fire. It was almost painful to feel so alive, so awake to her emotions, and yet she wanted more. She inhaled jaggedly as the fire crept along her veins, into her lungs, stealing her breath, as well.

She wasn't sure how long they danced. As suited the occasion, the orchestra was playing only movie themes, and the conductor, apparently aware that the late hour imparted a haze of sensuality to the room, offered one love song after another. Harps rippled; saxophones moaned; violins wept and sang. It was, Brooke thought as Taylor's chin drifted across her temple, almost too beautiful to bear.

Gradually, though, the dance floor began to clear, the other couples slipping away like sand emptying through an hourglass. Brooke shut her eyes again, turning her head into Taylor's jacket and tightening her arm on his shoulder, as if she could close the two of them inside a magic circle and make the evening last forever. She didn't want to go home, back to reality, back to all the problems that were waiting for her. She didn't think she could face being alone tonight.

With a sigh, she tucked their clasped hands under her cheek, letting her lips graze the back of his knuckles. His fingers tightened in response, and she felt oddly secure, here with his heart beating against her cheek. Strange, she mused. She'd been alone for years, but now, after spending less than an hour in this man's arms, she felt as if she had completely lost the knack.

He kissed the top of her head softly, and the flame inside her spread like a blossoming bud of heat. No, she didn't want to be alone. Not tonight.

"I think the orchestra is winding down," Taylor said, lifting his head and scanning the nearly empty stage. "It's getting late."

Without taking her cheek from his chest, she made a small, dismayed sound. But she didn't speak, afraid that her intense disappointment might sound fretful, as childish as Justin when he fussed about being sent to bed.

"You probably don't have a car here—do you want a taxi?" He feathered her hair back from her face and ducked his head lower, as if he were trying to get a glimpse of her expression. "Or would you like me to take you home?"

"Oh," she said, relief bringing a wide smile to her face as she lifted it toward him. "Oh, yes. Thank you."

He smiled, then, too, as if amused by her breathless eagerness, but she couldn't bring herself to care. What did it really matter if he could see how happy she was? What harm if he guessed how his embrace had made her feel?

Besides, even if she had wanted to, she wasn't sure she could have hidden her emotions. From the minute he'd put his arms around her, she had felt as if she'd been plugged into some vibrant life source. Illogically—especially considering that her problems were still unsolved, and Clarke, to whom she had looked for help, was long gone—she felt great. Better than great. She felt deliciously young and alive. Hot-blooded. And rapturously female.

So why not smile? If she was dwelling in a fool's paradise, then at least she would make the most of every minute. She'd been cautious every day of her life for the past ten years—and she'd have to be equally circumspect every day for the next ten.

Starting tomorrow.

She straightened, tugging lightly, eagerly, on his hand. "Yes," she said again, swiveling as she spoke. "Let's go home." After the warm cocoon of his arms, the cool air seemed to go straight to her head, and she felt the room tip slightly.

He chuckled, a low rumble that was more vibration than noise, and, pulling her safely back against his chest, kissed the tip of her nose. "Slowly," he said, steering her gently toward the stairs. "There's no need to rush."

But there was. There *was*. Couldn't he feel it, too? He kept his hands on her shoulders to steady her, and she tried to walk calmly, but a sense of urgency had suddenly overtaken her, like Cinderella as the clock began to strike midnight. If they didn't hurry, something could go wrong. The magic could run out. He could change his mind—or, even worse, she could change hers.

A crowd of late leavers clustered around the valet stand, and Brooke could hardly contain a sound of frustration. But Taylor's hands were still on her shoulders, pressing her back against the wall of his hard-muscled torso, and she leaned against him gratefully, glad that he was so strong, glad that he stood between her and the pushing, chattering crowd. She shut her eyes again, and she let herself imagine what it would be like to have such an ally in life, a partner whose strength and loyalty would be a seawall against the crashing waves of misfortune.

Time blipped erratically, and suddenly the car was there in front of them. It was a sleek steel gray model that she couldn't put a name to, though she could have made a pretty good guess at the price, which probably was approximately what she was asking for her bungalow. The irony of that struck her as rather funny, and she patted the hood of the car with a smile before letting Taylor guide her into the front seat.

Her cinnamon brown silk skirt made a sound like a sigh as it slid across the leather. Brooke sighed, too, as the air-conditioning blew sweet, cool air onto her cheeks, and when Taylor got in, she smiled at him. He smiled back, but his expression seemed strangely questioning.

"Oh," she said, suddenly realizing what he needed. "Sorry. I live at 909 Parker Lane." She peered through the window, trying to get her bearings. She knew downtown Tampa as well as she knew her own reflection in the mirror, but tonight things looked strangely unfamiliar. "Do you know where it is, by any chance?" She knew she sounded dubious, but where exactly *were* they? She didn't recognize that huge building. "I can navigate, I suppose, as long as you don't drive too fast—"

"You rest," he said, touching her face. He wasn't smiling anymore, but it sounded somehow as if the smile was tucked inside his voice. He sounded sexy, affectionate...and kind. "I'm sure I can find it."

"That's good," she murmured, shutting her eyes against the bright blur of streetlights as they swept down the nearly deserted boulevard. "I'm a little tired. Look for roses. I have a lot of roses in the front...."

He put his arm across the back of the seat and, closing his palm over her shoulder, nudged her gently.

"Rest," he said again, and she felt no urge to protest as he eased her toward him. She let herself drift downward slowly, her head seeming to seek the crook of his arm as if it were her own special spot, her assigned place in the universe. She put her hand on his thigh, registering the lean, solid strength of it somewhere in the back of her mind before she closed her eyes again and kept drifting, but this time father and farther, until she was so far away—

"Taylor," she said suddenly, though she didn't open her eyes, "we've never met before, have we?"

His voice was right next to her ear. Strange, when she'd thought she had floated so very far away. "No," he said huskily, "we've never met before."

"Are you sure? You feel so...familiar."

He didn't answer for a long moment, and when he did she heard a smile in his voice. "I have a rather nutty friend who would say that means our auras are in harmony. Maybe he's right."

She smiled, too, still without opening her eyes. "That's silly."

He stroked her arm gently. "I always used to think so."

"Very silly." She shook her head—or at least she thought she did. Her voice sounded thick, half-asleep. "Still, you're not really a stranger, Taylor. I know you're not a stranger."

CHAPTER THREE

SHE came to consciousness achingly aware of him, of his hand stroking along her temple, into her hair, all the way behind her ear. They were home—she could smell the thick scent of roses in her own, beloved front garden. She had been asleep, but the short reprieve into unconsciousness hadn't helped to clear her head. She was still racked with a shivering desire for this man who sat beside her.

His hand kept moving, and her skin prickled with tiny bumps, from the ear he traced, down her neck and deep into the core of her. Heat was shifting inside her, pulsing and coiling and demanding things she had forgotten were possible.

"Taylor." She turned her face into his jacket, nuzzling for a deeper connection, and moved her hand on his thigh, letting her fingers tell him what she didn't know how to say. She wanted him. Oh, God help her, how she wanted him!

The long muscle in his leg tensed, and his fingers tunneled into her hair. "Hi, sleepyhead." His voice was husky, as if he had been sitting out here in the night air a long time. "Ready to go in?"

She nodded, her pulse beating so hard against her throat that she wasn't sure she could speak.

He lifted his arm, giving her the freedom to rise, but she didn't move away, reluctant to surrender the warmth of him. She tilted her face toward his, searching his rugged, elegant features, gilded now by the soft light of her front pillar lanterns. He had angled his head to face her, and his eyes shimmered, bottomless green-and-gold depths rimmed in thick, dusky black fringe. Their gazes held silently for a long moment, during which her lips parted, and even his breathing took on a subtly rougher cant.

"Brooke," he said slowly, letting his arm drop across her again. His fingers massaged the sensitive skin above her collarbone. "Do you know how beautiful you are right now?"

"Am I?" Though she knew it wasn't true, for to-night—for him—she wanted to be. She wanted to possess the kind of beauty that could hypnotize a man, could throw a silken net around him and hold him captive. "Am I?"

For answer, his hand tightened, his thumb rubbing against her neck. His eyes were heavy with sensuality, but she could still see the gold flecks that sparked like tiny fires beneath his lowered lids. "Yes, you are," he murmured. "Dangerously beautiful."

She watched his full lips form the words, and without conscious thought she lifted her mouth, which tingled with anticipation. But, to her disappointment, he simply dragged in a deep breath, and moving with a stiffness that spoke of rigid determination, he moved away, got out of the car and held open the door for her.

She slid out with a sudden numbness, wondering what his abrupt withdrawal could mean. She couldn't think how to ask, so she busied herself digging out the key from her evening bag as they made their way up to the house. He seemed to sense that her balance was still rocky—he walked close, close enough to reassure her as they climbed the four steep steps to her front porch.

Once there, her mind raced in circles. If she didn't think of something quickly, it was going to be too late. Helplessly, she twisted the key in the lock, and then she turned to him.

"Taylor—" she put her hand on his arm "—don't you want to come in? Just for a little while?" What was the polite euphemism? She didn't do this kind of thing, didn't know what the rules were. "For a cup of coffee?"

The muscle in his forearm shifted and grew brick hard under her fingers. She looked up at him, confused. The look in his green eyes was equally hard. "If I come in, Brooke," he said with a flat monotone, "it won't be for coffee. We both know that."

"I..." She licked her dry lips and tried to think of the right answer. But her mind wasn't working. He was going to leave her here with this empty loneliness that had suddenly become unbearable—that was all she knew clearly. "I just don't want to be alone," she said, her voice cracking on the last word stupidly, pitifully. She felt a flare of embarrassment at the sound. What must he think? If he didn't want to come in, then she was making herself ridiculous.

But suddenly, in spite of her efforts, her eyes were full of tears, and he was just a blurred outline in the lantern light. Mortified, she pulled her hand from his arm and pressed her fingers on either side of her nose, trying to hold the tears back. Oh, what a fool she was! What had she thought? That just because he had been kind to her, because she had absurdly imagined some sense of inexplicable familiarity, because she found him, his body, his face, his touch, somehow deeply moving... Had she really believed that he felt the same way?

"I'm sorry," she said, turning away. She fumbled for the living-room light, but everything was wet and glimmering, and she gave up quickly. "Thank you for all your help—"

"Damn it—Brooke..." He grabbed her arm, his voice a harsh, urgent whisper. With two rough steps he was beside her in the darkness, pulling her against him, his hands hard on her back. The door swung shut behind them, and everything went black. "Brooke," he said again, more gently, and he kissed the edge of her lips. She felt herself softening, sinking into him, like rain disappearing into the earth. His mouth slanted over hers, poised and warm, grazing her as he whispered, "Brooke, why are you crying? Don't you know how much I want you?"

She shook her head once, a half movement that barely stirred the darkness. But he must have seen, because suddenly, with a low groan, he dragged her up against him and kissed her again, but deeply this time, as if he could pour into her his proof, as if she could drink understanding from his lips.

And she did. She did. With a half-smothered cry of joy, she lifted her arms and wrapped them around his neck. Though the room was dark, she shut her eyes so that nothing was real except his kiss. It was sweet, but with a burning, like an exotic liqueur. It spread through her limbs, hot and potent, washing her, melting her, until she was limp and clinging, liquid in his arms.

Finally, Taylor drew back, but only an inch. His breath was still sweet and warm on her cheeks. "Where is your son?"

The question was clear, and she didn't pretend she didn't understand. "He sleeps upstairs, next to his nurse." She swallowed. "My room is downstairs. I'm not usually...not usually home at night."

He didn't answer. Suddenly, the darkness spun, shadows moving on shadows, as he scooped her up and carried her through the living room, deeper into the house. It was a small home, with few options for privacy. He paused at the only shut door, the door to her bedroom, and somehow she knew this silent hesitation would be his last question. Her heart pounding in her throat, she minutely nodded her head, trying not to think of the implications of that tiny movement. She felt his pectoral muscles shift under her cheek as he shouldered the door open with the smooth assurance of a man who didn't give a damn for implications.

The room smelled of roses as it always did—she kept cut blooms in a vase by her bed. But never before had the fragrance seemed so heavy, red and sensual. Still without speaking, he laid her on the cool satin tufts of her quilted bedspread, and she could feel herself sinking, sinking endlessly into its perfumed softness. Opening her eyes, she focused on the dark, featureless silhouette of his head, clutching the edges of his jacket in trembling fingers, afraid that she might lose him in this slow, bottomless descent.

Kneeling in front of her, he kissed her again, and again and again, his mouth moving on hers with infinite variety—soft, then harder, angling from corner to corner, then coming full center, feathering lightly, then plundering deeply. It was, in some wonderful way, like talking—he was telling her things she'd never guessed, promising her things she'd always wanted. But it was better than words because she didn't have to think, didn't have to struggle to find the right reply. She could simply give herself over to feeling. It was so beautifully simple. She opened her lips and met his urgent questions with equally primal answers.

When he lifted her, reaching beneath her shoulders to slide open the zipper of her dress, that seemed simple, too. She nuzzled the hollow of his shoulder, kissing the pulse that beat there, and then lay back obediently as he slipped the cool silk down her arms, dragging a trail of goose bumps along her skin. When she was free, he touched her naked breasts with his lips, and she moaned softly, a low, quavering sound that purled through the darkness like the ripple of a harp.

He suckled her, the act so intimate, so powerful that she cried out at the piercing beauty of it and pressed his head to her with trembling fingers, needing more, begging for more.

"Oh, yes," she whispered as he took her deeper. It felt so miraculously natural, his teeth grazing her nipple, his quick breath warm against her breast, his hair a silken tickle against her skin. He seemed to pull some mysterious female essence from her soul.

Strangely, she felt no shame, though it had been such a long, frozen time since any man had touched her. Ten years... And it hadn't been a man, not back then. It had been a boy. A sweet boy, who would have liked to please her, who had tried for long, awkward minutes to coax out of her untutored body even a hint of this melting pleasure.

And she had been only a girl, a lonely, ignorant girl. Working so hard, tense and straining, wanting to make it easy for him, knowing there should be more but unable to find the key that would unlock the magic. She thought she would cry now, thinking of that girl who had never felt like this.

It was so sublimely different here, in this swirling darkness that smelled of her bedside roses, with this sensual man whose presence in her bedroom was so inexplicably right. No effort was needed, no clumsy straining. It was as if she were floating on some hot, bucking current, swept forcefully along toward a final, shattering perfection that waited just beyond the darkness. Taylor's mouth was everywhere, rising to claim her tingling lips again, then back down to her swollen, aching breasts, feathering kisses along the path of sensitive skin between. And his hands, his hands...

She gasped, arching, as he placed his palm gently between her legs, cupping her at the white-fire center of all sensation. She whimpered, unable to bear the throbbing pleasure that radiated out from his fingers, up into her belly and down into her legs. He was lying beside her, and she clutched frantically at his forearm. Now that the moment was finally here, she was afraid. She had waited ten years for this....

"Shhh," he said softly as she whimpered again. His lips were right next to her ear, his breath a tormenting tease of heat that daggered through her. "Just relax and let it happen, sweetheart. You're ready."

She tried to obey. But even as she subsided in his arms, he began to increase the pressure, slowly but surely, pushing the heel of his hand ever more firmly against her, until the pinpoint of need seemed to throb violently against him. She made another small, desperate noise, helpless to prevent it from escaping through her open, panting lips. He sucked slowly, sensuously, on the lobe of her ear and pressed harder.

It was too much to bear. She twisted under his hand helplessly, seeking release. Every nerve in her body seemed to concentrate in that one pulsing spot, and she knew that he was right—she was ready. Ready to surrender all her tension, all her worries and her fears. Ready to let him take her away from this tired, lonely world into another space and time, another place so full of life and peace and beauty that, for one triumphant moment, she would be utterly and magically free.

"I want this," she said, though she hardly had the breath to speak. She twisted under his hand again and groaned at the perfect pain. "I want this so much."

"I know," he whispered, and then he groaned, too, as if he needed it as much as she did. Finally, the rigid stillness of his hand gave way to a deft and fluid urging, his palm rotating slightly, taking up the rhythm her frantic body was trying to find.

She cried out as the darkness began to spiral away from her, strobe flashes of blinding light filling her vision, jagged streaks of black lightning stabbing through her body. He slipped two fingers into her, and, as if that was the signal her body had been waiting for, she finally lifted free of her body and, with a deafening internal tremor, ascended like a sparkling column of fire into a place that felt a lot like heaven.

* * *

When she woke again, it was with an oppressive sense that something was wrong. Something new, something darkly sexual hung in the shadows like smoke, invisibly thickening the air she breathed. She sat up, wrapping one arm protectively around her naked breasts, though instinctively she sensed she was alone, and peered into the darkness. Alone, that is, except for this strange miasma of sexuality.

She rubbed her eyes with two fingertips, trying to orient herself. Where was Taylor? He should be here, shouldn't he? She remembered well—too well for comfort—that he had carried her here, had placed her on the bed, undressed her, touched her....

And then she had fallen asleep. A deep embarrassment flushed through her like warm water as she remembered everything. Half-drunk and soul-weary, she had let him bring her to a shattering climax, and then, lulled by a more delicious peace than she had ever known in her life, she had curled up in his arms and fallen asleep.

She dropped her face into her hands. Fallen asleep! She could only imagine what he must think of her, taking her satisfaction and ignoring his. He couldn't know that it was something she'd never experienced before—something she'd given up hope of ever finding.

She stood up quickly and traversed the black shadows toward her closet, reached in and grabbed the first thing that met her fingers, though it was an old, faded oversize T-shirt so stretched out of shape it slipped precariously over one shoulder. Hardly the uniform of seduction.

But there wasn't time for anything more glamorous. Where *was* he? Could he have left without even saying goodbye? Pulling the shirt over her head, she hurried to the window and nudged the drapes apart a quarter of an inch. His car was still there, gleaming like black ice in the lamplight. Blind relief shimmered along her veins. He hadn't left her. He was still here.

But where? In the kitchen, perhaps? When he had brought her home, they hadn't even taken time for the perfunctory amenities. No cup of coffee, no chitchat in the living room. Perhaps, she thought distractedly, she could remedy that now.

She went out into the dimly lit hall, listening for sounds that might lead her to him without calling out. She didn't want to wake Gretchen, though thank goodness the older woman was a sound sleeper. God only knew what Gretchen would make of Brooke's appearance—the smudged makeup, the T-shirt hastily draped over her nakedness, the disheveled hair.

Self-consciously, Brooke tried to run her fingers through her hair as she walked, but she encountered a tangle at the back, a knot of matted strands so impenetrable her fingers snagged. A new wave of embarrassment flushed through her as she imagined how such a knot had been formed. She must have been completely abandoned. She must have been tossing her head restlessly, frantically, on the pillow while he...

She leaned against the wall, suddenly weak-kneed as, alongside the embarrassment, a new sensation bloomed. A burgeoning desire pressed swollenly against her skin, from her throbbing heart to her tingling knees, as if her body were too small to contain it. Tilting her head back, she shut her eyes, remembering. Dear God, it had been wonderful, hadn't it? No wonder men committed such madness in the name of love. It was... She swallowed and crossed her hands over her stomach. It was ravishing.

No light winked from beneath the closed bathroom door. The kitchen was dark and silent. Even the living room had the quiet, stale air of a completely empty room. She walked silently across the carpet toward the stairs, her heartbeat instinctively accelerating. Where could he be? She glanced out the front window, nervously confirming that his car was really there, that she hadn't dreamed it. Yes. The expensive machine still hugged the curb.

So...where was Taylor?

She hesitated at the foot of the stairs, looking up to where the creamy night-light illuminated a small vase of flowers picked from the backyard garden. She stared blankly, disbelieving her own thoughts. Surely he wouldn't have gone upstairs, not in a total stranger's house, not when he knew Justin's nursery was up there, that the little boy was sleeping....

Suddenly, at the thought of her son, a jolt of adrenaline surged through her, and her feet began to fly up the wooden staircase. Her heart seemed to press against her throat. *Justin*, she said inwardly, over and over. *Justin*.

At the head of the stairs, she stopped, her hand wrapped around the newel post so tightly her fingertips were white. Justin's nursery was at the end of the short hall, and the door to the little blue room was open. Taylor stood just beside the crib, a black shadow silhouetted in the glow from the small table lamp. The mobile of terry-cloth zoo animals that hung over Justin's head jiggled erratically, as if someone had just jostled it—but Taylor himself was ominously still, his hands braced against the safety bar, his head bent slightly as he stared down into the crib.

Something in his posture, some quality of brooding intensity, was wrong, she thought hazily. Suddenly, Brooke tasted the metallic flavor of fear, and her breathing sounded like a roar in her ears. What was he doing up here? What did he want with Justin?

She forced herself to walk forward slowly, quietly, passing Gretchen's room without making a sound that might awaken the older woman. Her bare feet were numb, but somehow she managed not to stumble over the bunny pull toy that had been left in the center of the hall. She had almost reached the door to Justin's room when, in her anxious haste, she elbowed a brightly colored velveteen ball from the telephone table. It fell to the floor with the muffled, chiming *plink-plonk* that always made Justin laugh.

She froze, watching the silhouette in the doorway for a reaction, but there was none. Taylor stood as still as ever and stared unblinking into the crib. Somehow, Brooke thought, watching him, his lack of a reaction was the most disturbing thing of all. It was as if he knew, had always known, that she was approaching. It was as if he was patiently, almost grimly, waiting for her to join him.

Somehow, with a supreme effort of will, she got as far as the doorway, and then she stopped. Her knees were weak, and goose bumps prickled along her shoulder where the T-shirt had drooped away.

"That's Justin," she said, though she knew it was idiotic, the overobvious. But she could hardly burst in screaming, ordering him to get away from her little boy. He hadn't *done* anything, had he? He was just standing there, looking, watching. Waiting.

She had to stay calm—surely that was her best course, whether he had good motives or bad. She looked at him, sickeningly confused, suddenly guilty. She had let him in. A stranger...

But how *could* he have evil in his heart, this man who had been so kind to her? She shook the thought away. She must give him time to explain. She had to act...normal. But what, she wondered, could she possibly say that would sound normal in such an abnormal situation?

"My son," she elucidated stupidly. Her voice was strained, cracking as she forced the words through her dry, narrowed windpipe. She pushed herself into the room. Act normal. And surely, after nearly making love with this man just minutes ago, her most normal move would be to go to him, touch his hand, smile into his handsome face....

Her legs would hardly carry her. She reached his side with her heart thudding wildly against her rib cage. She tried to breathe evenly, tried to smile as she, too, looked down at the sleeping little boy. "He's just turned two," she said, gripping the bars of the crib hard. "He's a darling, isn't he?"

Finally, Taylor stirred beside her. She looked up, hope and dread fighting for control of her pounding heart. There was some barely restrained emotion, something that felt strangely like anger, in the quick, jerking motion of his head as he nodded.

"Yes," he said, the word stiff and sibilant in the midnight silence. "Yes, he's a beautiful child." He raised his head finally, and his gaze locked hard with hers. "But he's *mine*."

CHAPTER FOUR

FOR a long, blank moment, Brooke stared at him. It had been such a simple sentence, merely three little words, and yet it made no sense at all. Justin, *his*? Why on earth would he say such a thing? It was impossible. Worse than impossible—it was crazy. Taylor had never seen Justin before, had never even set foot in this house before.

Perhaps she had misheard him. But the words hung in the air, as visible as if they had been written in neon. *He's mine*. Her mind reeled—what could he mean? The sentence itself was a startling non sequitur, but the way he had said it was even more disturbing. Grim. Flat. Tense. A primitive fear prickled along her spine, and operating from sheer instinct, she reached into the crib and scooped Justin's sleeping form into her arms, which she willed not to shake.

The little boy half opened his eyes and lifted his head, whimpering a complaint at being disturbed, but Brooke held him tightly against her chest, and soon he subsided, nuzzling his forehead against her shoulder, then falling promptly back to sleep. His body was warm from being blanketed all night, and his hair was moist along his neck. Brooke pressed him closer, taking comfort from the warmth.

Finally, squaring her shoulders, she looked up, and she knew a hint of trembling defiance was visible in the clenched set of her jaw. If there was danger, she would protect Justin from it, no matter what. She was not afraid.

"I don't know what you're doing up here," she said, her voice throbbing with something that sounded, even to her own ears, exactly like fear. She toughened it as best she could. Better, she decided frantically, to sound rude than vulnerable. "I want you to leave this room right now. We can talk downstairs. You're frightening Justin."

Taylor looked at the sleeping child, then lifted his piercing green gaze to Brooke. "He's not frightened, Brooke. Frankly, it sounds as if *you* are." He moved closer. "Why would you be frightened? Is it because you're feeling a little guilty?"

"Guilty? Why would I feel guilty?" In spite of her determination to stand firm, Brooke felt herself backing away from the intimidating power of the man. She had gained only a foot or so before her spine rammed into the rails of the crib, shaking a couple of eerie, tinkling notes loose from the musical mobile. She never took her eyes from Taylor, whose face was a strange mask of shadows and lamplight, though his eyes seemed to bore into her. "I'm not the one prowling around someone else's house in the middle of the night like a thief."

For a minute, she thought the insult had hit home. He narrowed his eyes, and his hands made fists at his sides. But he recovered quickly.

"No," he agreed, again moving slowly closer. "But maybe you're feeling guilty because you know—or at least suspect—that I'm telling the truth. Maybe you've always known that Justin isn't rightfully yours." He spoke as slowly as he moved, and the effect was rather chilling. "Maybe you know there's someone else who has a stronger claim. A legitimate claim, Brooke. A blood claim."

He was very close now. Too close. She was breathlessly aware of the lean strength of his powerful body. Just under her chin, she could feel the small, rhythmic motion of Justin's lips as he found his fist and sucked on it. The little boy rarely sucked his fingers anymore, except when he was in pain, and Brooke knew she must be squeezing him too tightly. She tried to relax her hold, but her arms clutched with a panic that was beyond reason.

Swallowing hard, she forced herself to meet Taylor's darkly burning gaze. Oh, God, what had she done? Why had she brought him here? Why had she allowed herself to forget that this man was a total stranger, no matter how suave, no matter how handsome, no matter how—

No matter how oddly familiar his gaze might be.

"You're misinformed." Brooke tried to sound calm and forceful, tried not to let that strange, niggling doubt undermine her confidence. But why—why were his eyes so familiar? "Justin is my son. *My* son. And you have no right to be up here. I'm asking you to leave right now. If you don't, I'll call the police."

He didn't look at all intimidated. "Go ahead and call them, Brooke. Call the whole state militia if you'd like. He's mine, and I can prove it."

Her heartbeat accelerated. Prove it? How? But he sounded so certain—so terrifyingly certain that even Brooke herself, who had wept at the graveside of Justin's parents, holding the orphaned infant in her arms, who had placed the finalized adoption papers securely in her safe-deposit box, who had tucked Justin into this very crib every night for the past two years, suddenly doubted the facts. It was like being in the epicenter of a nightmare, as if the solid ground of truth were shifting under her feet.

"You're wrong," she said again, but this time her voice was thin and strained. "I assure you that Justin is legally mine. I adopted him almost two years ago when he was only an infant. Both his parents are dead, and he had no relatives who wanted him. He had only the two uncles, and they were quite happy to let him go—"

"No, Brooke." Taylor was shaking his head slowly.

She stared at him, bewildered. "Yes," she insisted. "Yes—they both signed their rights away eagerly—"

"No." He was implacable. "Not both of them."

She felt suddenly light-headed. She tried to drag in a deep breath, but her chest hurt as if the small, pointed sentence were a poisoned dagger lodged in her breast.

Oh, God... Her breath was ragged, loud in the spinning silence. Oh, God...

She thought for a moment she might faint, but Taylor's deep-set green eyes mesmerized her. Catching the light from the bedside lamp, they seemed, like eyes in a movie, to glow with a strange, compelling force. Eyes as green as emeralds, striated with streaks of gold, fringed in thick, black lashes. It had been the eyes all along, she realized. Those wonderful, sexy eyes had seemed so comfortingly familiar, so deceptively like the eyes of someone she knew, someone she trusted, someone she *loved*.

And then, with a hawklike swoop that seemed to pluck the breath from her lungs, the truth descended on her. She *knew*. They were Justin's eyes.

He's mine. All her muscles went weak, and Justin slipped in her arms before she secured him desperately against her breast. It was true. This man was related to Justin, was connected to him by a genetic bond so strong and pure that the two green-eyed males could have been identified as kin by anyone who saw them together.

And that was why Taylor had come here. Not because he was her knight in shining armor, rescuing her from Clarke. Not because he was enchanted with her pretty party dress or because he admired her graceful dancing. Not even because he wanted to bed her. He had come here to see Justin.

To take Justin away from her.

"Oh, dear God..." Brooke slid to one side, stumbling backward, clutching Justin so tightly he finally awakened and began to fuss. Clumsy in her confusion, she encountered the edge of the door, inadvertently banging it shut, locking them into the intense isolation of the tiny nursery.

At the sound, Justin lifted his head, dazed and irritable, and twisted around, trying to get his bearings. When he saw Taylor, a dark and glowering stranger standing beside his crib, he buried his head in Brooke's breast and began to wail in earnest.

"Go away!" she cried over the din, finally too overwrought to control her fear. "Can't you see you're frightening him? He's afraid of strange men!"

Brooke saw the immediate recoil in Taylor's body, the deep flush that darkened his strong features. He started to move toward her, but at that moment Gretchen shoved open the door, her chenille robe clutched high at her neck with one hand and the other hand wrapped around the base of a heavy brass candlestick. She obviously had been roused from a deep sleep—gray hair fell raggedly out of pin curls, and her eyes, though full of fear, were puffy, slightly disoriented.

But as the older woman took in the strange scene before her—Justin weeping, Brooke obviously naked under her skimpy T-shirt, the handsome man in his impeccable tuxedo—the candlestick, which she had been brandishing at shoulder level, slowly fell to her side.

"Brooke?" Gretchen said tentatively, tucking the candlestick behind her back, blushing all the way to her ears. "I'm sorry...I...heard noises...."

"It's all right, Gretchen," Brooke tried to say, but Justin had begun to scream, no doubt alarmed by the chaos and the fear he must have sensed in his mother's tense and clutching arms. He writhed, trying to free himself, kicking his ceramic piggy bank from the dresser with an angry foot. As it crashed to the floor, the bank splintered into a thousand shards, raining coins, and the sound only made him scream harder. Brooke groaned,

trying to hold him still without hurting his skin grafts.
Oh, God, it was bedlam.

"Yes, it's all right, Gretchen," Taylor said, his deep
voice somehow managing to master the madness. "I was
just leaving."

He strode past the insane scene toward the door, not
deigning to look at either of the women. Gretchen sidled
out of his way, instinctively deferring to the imposing
stranger she had only minutes ago intended to club with
a candlestick.

At the doorway, he turned back, his body rigid, his
face tight.

"Goddamn it, Brooke," he said between his teeth,
"I'm not a stranger." Brooke met his gaze, and with a
jolt she remembered the sleepy intuition she had felt
earlier, the subconscious recognition that had led her to
whisper the same words as she rested her head against
his heart. No, he was not a stranger.... Against her will,
she remembered, too, the thrill of his hands on her body.
It had seemed so wonderful, so simple and good. How
could it have come to this?

She watched him in mute misery, knowing what he
was about to say, wishing she could somehow stop time
in its tracks. Or better still, turn back the clock, go back
to the innocent rapture of only an hour ago, when he
had seemed like a gift sent to her by a beneficent fate.

But she was helpless. Nothing could stem the frustrated fury she felt flowing from him. Nothing could
stop the words he was determined to say.

"I'm not a stranger," he repeated coldly. "I'm his
uncle. My lawyer will call you in the morning."

A week later, Brooke sat in a large, well-appointed office
surrounded by three very expensive lawyers, not one of
whom, it seemed, was going to be able to help her one
bit, though they'd spent the past seven days trying and
would undoubtedly bill her for every minute of it.

"So what you're saying," she said, attempting to sound calm, though the knuckles were white on the hands she kept neatly folded in her lap, "is that if Taylor Pryce takes me to court for custody of Justin, you can't be at all sure I'll win."

Malcolm Ingress, the middle-aged adoption lawyer who sat behind the big desk, made circles on the arm of his chair with the eraser end of his pencil. "You're never *sure* you'll win when you go to court," he said patiently, as if he were talking to a child. "Any lawyer who promises to win isn't being quite honest."

Brooke mentally counted to ten. "I know that, Mr. Ingress," she said, and she was proud of her neutral tone. None of these men would guess, she was sure, that she felt humiliated, terrified and furious. "I meant that you don't think my chances are very good in this particular case."

Clarke Westover, who had been pacing in front of the wall of bookshelves, irritably shoving red-leather volumes in and out, looked up at that. His face was red, his features distorted, and Brooke knew she had finally given him the opening he'd been waiting for.

"Your chances would be a damned sight better," Clarke spat out, "if you hadn't been in such a hurry to bring a total stranger back to your house last Friday night."

Brooke tried not to flush, but her cheekbones felt uncomfortably hot in spite of her best efforts. "Then perhaps you shouldn't have left me at the theater alone," she said, and suddenly the heat was in her voice, too. "What was I supposed to do? I didn't know a soul in that room, Clarke. I didn't even have a ride home."

"So Taylor Pryce was just transportation?" Clarke made a guttural sound. "Tell me, Brooke, does every man who gives you a ride home get to sleep with you?"

The third lawyer, Julien Matheson, a white-haired man who specialized in child custody suits, held up a restraining hand. "Really, Westover," he said, "that's a bit much."

Brooke watched as Clarke swallowed some of his anger. But there was plenty left, and it showed in the pinched quality of his voice. "Well, it's no more than Taylor Pryce and his lawyers are going to say, Matheson, and you know it. They're going to be screaming 'morally unfit' at the top of their legal lungs."

Brooke half rose, indignation streaking through her like a jolt of electricity. "Morally unfit?" she echoed disbelievingly. "That's absurd. I'm not in the habit of— of..." She could hardly say the word. "Of sleeping with strange men. I've never done such a thing before in my life. And what about Taylor himself? If I took a strange man to my home, then he went home with a strange woman, didn't he? Doesn't that make *him* as guilty as I am?" She frowned at the men. Except for Clarke, their faces were reserved, the features of skilled poker players. "Good grief," she expostulated. "Isn't this the twentieth century?"

Matheson shook his courtly white head sadly. "Not in custody cases," he said with an apologetic air. "Unfortunately, there's still something of a double standard."

"But—"

"And besides," Clarke interjected with a nasty tone, "Taylor's morals, or lack thereof, didn't jeopardize the child, did they? He didn't open up his bedroom to a total stranger and then fall asleep, leaving Justin completely unprotected." He watched Brooke subside into her chair as his words sank in. His expression had changed, she noted dully, to an unpleasant smirk of triumph. "That's the reality of it, Brooke. You're damned lucky he didn't murder you all in your beds."

He was right. Brooke had no answer, no defense at all, and she didn't try to offer one. Clarke would never forgive her for what had happened, and she knew why. He had never really loved her, but he had wanted to be her lover so desperately that he had been willing to make her his wife. He had tried for two years, with every enticement he could think of, from flattery to trinkets and finally to diamonds, to coax her into bed. All in vain—and now it infuriated him to realize that she had openly offered that intimacy to a total stranger.

Yes, it was Taylor's easy success that had mortally insulted Clarke, even more than his own failure. Where once there had been resentment, now there was hatred.

And she had done this all to herself. She stared at her twined fingers, wishing, as she had wished every moment since that night, that she could go back and change everything. She wouldn't have danced with Taylor, wouldn't have put her head against his chest, wouldn't have kissed him at the door...

But she couldn't change the past. And now these men were telling her she might lose her son because of it.

"So what do you suggest I do?" She encompassed all three men in her questioning gaze. "I refuse to simply hand Justin over to this man. If Taylor Pryce had come forward after the bombing and wanted his nephew, I would never have dreamed of standing in his way. But instead he signed away his rights—"

"He says he didn't, you know," Matheson broke in. "He says the signature is a forgery."

The lawyer's voice was perfectly flat and factual, his tone revealing nothing. And yet, looking at his bland, self-satisfied face, Brooke was suddenly quite sure that, in their patriarchal hearts, all three lawyers secretly thought that Taylor was telling the truth. It wouldn't stop them from representing her, of course, and representing her as well as they could...for the right price. But they had clearly made up their minds already. Their logic was simple: Taylor was a rich, male professional. One of them. Ergo, he was by birth entitled to whatever he wanted.

"Well, I don't believe him," Brooke said, frustration sharpening her voice. At what she was paying them, they should be on her side, damn it. "He's already proved himself a liar. You heard him the other night at the auction, didn't you, Clarke? He said his name was Taylor Allen."

"And it is," Matheson interjected again, as smoothly as ever. "Taylor Allen Pryce. He signed in that way—we've checked the guest book. Apparently it was the auctioneer who got it wrong." He leaned forward, arranging his face in a textbook example of paternal sympathy. "Be reasonable, Brooke. You're grasping at straws here, and of course that's understandable. We all know how upset you must be at the thought of losing Justin—"

"I will *not* lose him," she bit out, rising to her feet on a geyser of panic and anger. She pressed her fists to her breastbone as if to contain the fear that beat wildly against her rib cage. "Justin is my son." Her voice broke on the last word. "My son. Do you understand what that means? I won't lose him. I can't."

Another uneasy silence settled over the three men. It was Clarke who finally broke it. "You may not have any choice," he said. "Matheson and Ingress are trying to spare your feelings, but the bottom line is Pryce is blood kin, and you're not. You'll be lucky if we can get you joint custody."

She spun toward Clarke, infuriated by the gloating undertone in his voice. "Then perhaps I should get myself another lawyer," she said tightly. "After all, you are the ones who drew up my adoption papers. Apparently they're not exactly airtight, are they?"

"And that's why we're willing to take this case for such a minimal fee." Clarke flattened his lips in a sneer, obviously relishing the opportunity to remind Brooke that what seemed like a fortune to her was peanuts to them. And that she could hardly afford to go elsewhere. "We feel a certain responsibility."

At that, Ingress cleared his throat and held up a cautionary finger. "A certain 'sympathetic interest' would perhaps be a better way to put it, Westover." He flashed a patently false smile toward Brooke. "We wouldn't want to imply that the firm has any liability in this matter."

Of course not. Heaven forbid that these smug, complacent lawyers should be held responsible for wrecking a two-year-old child's life. Or for breaking a young woman's heart. And suddenly, with a flash of sickening insight, she saw what their real agenda was. They didn't care about her or Justin, or even Taylor Pryce. They only cared about covering their own designer-clad backsides. As long as neither of the parties became disgruntled enough to file a suit against them, these men didn't give a tinker's damn who got the child.

An overwhelming sense of exhaustion swept through her. Her legs felt so uncertain that she had to touch the top of Malcolm's glossy desk to balance herself. She rubbed her other hand across her aching eyes.

"This is crazy," she said numbly, trying to fight the fatalistic feeling that threatened to overtake her. She was way out of her league here. She was just a mother who loved her little boy and who desperately wanted him to be happy. Why couldn't it be that simple? She didn't know anything about lawsuits and power plays and good-old-boy clubs where everyone protected everyone else as long as they had the correct chromosome configuration. "Maybe I should just talk to Taylor myself—"

The room erupted. Julien emitted a quiet groan, and Malcolm shook his head vehemently. "For God's sake, don't do that," he blurted.

Even Clarke looked uncomfortable. "Listen to me, Brooke," he said, his voice agitated. "That would be the worst possible thing you could do at this point. You mustn't spend another minute alone with that man. You haven't got an ounce of judgment where Taylor Pryce is concerned. God knows what he could get you to say."

She glanced up, something not quite defeated sparking in her breast. "It isn't what I might *say* that frightens you, is it, Clarke? It's what I might *do*."

He tilted his chin so that he ended up looking at her down the length of his patrician nose. "You've already shown us what you'll *do*," he said with a slicing sarcasm. "But if you think you can use your...charms...to bargain with Taylor Pryce, my guess is that you've misjudged the man."

Her cheeks stung as if he had slapped her. She straightened and faced him squarely.

"Well, he won't be the first man I've misjudged, Clarke," she said in a quietly fierce undertone. "As I recall, I once thought rather highly of you, too."

Taylor sighed as the masseuse began to work on his shoulders. Mindy's talented fingers seemed to force the warm oil all the way into his muscles, slowly loosening them. He shifted on the table, consciously relaxing his neck. God, he needed this. Over the past week, his body had coiled tighter and tighter, until he had begun to feel as if he were made of an interlocking system of steel cables rather than flesh and blood.

Thankfully, though she was indisputably decorative, Mindy wasn't just someone the hotel had hired for show. She was a trained masseuse, and she meant business. Her fingers found every knot as if guided by radar, then closed in, kneading so deeply that the pain screamed through Taylor's body.

The good news was that it almost drowned out Charlie's continuing tirade from the sofa by the sitting-room window. Almost.

Taylor shut his eyes, riding each pain until it broke and dissolved, no longer really trying to follow Charlie's words. The lawyer had run out of steam several minutes ago—he was just repeating himself now, frustrated that he hadn't been able to jolt a satisfactory reaction out of Taylor.

A few tones and phrases drifted into Taylor's consciousness around the signals his muscles were sending. Incredulity was still Charlie's dominant theme. "I just can't believe you did that." With a strong note of regret, "...shouldn't ever have given you her address." And always, underlying it all, indignation. "...beneath you, Taylor, really it was."

Finished for the moment with his shoulders, Mindy moved to his arm. The pain backed off a little. But Charlie was still fussing and fuming.

"Tell me something, McAllister," Taylor broke in without opening his eyes. "Were you always such a prig?"

A small silence hung heavily. "I don't know," Charlie answered slowly. "Were you always such a villain?"

Mindy's hands hesitated slightly, as if she expected Taylor to do something dramatic in response to the insult. When he didn't, she resumed her rhythmic kneading without comment, the ultimate deaf-and-dumb professional. Taylor lifted languidly up on the elbow she didn't need and raised his brows at Charlie.

"A villain? Aren't you crossing the line into melodrama here, pal? What exactly do you think I did? Do you think I tied Brooke Davenport to the bed and ravished her to within an inch of her life?"

Charlie flushed. "I know what you did. I've talked to her lawyers, remember?"

"Well, then, you should be well aware that anything Brooke did that night she did of her own free will."

"Free will, my foot." Charlie pointed an accusing finger at Taylor. "You knew she'd been drinking."

Taylor laughed, one corner of his mouth twisting cynically. "I hope she's not planning to use *that* as a defense."

"And she didn't know who you really were."

Taylor shrugged. "Even worse."

"Damn it, Taylor, we're not in court now. I'm saying it was a nasty trick. It was cheap and coldhearted, and frankly, speaking as a lawyer, I think it may have been entrapment. You went there with the express purpose of tricking her into having sex with you and—"

"For the tenth time, Charlie, we didn't have sex."

Charlie's lips pressed together tightly. "Merely a technicality," he said. "Both morally and legally."

Taylor sighed again and lay back down. He didn't suppose it would do any good to protest that he had *not* planned to take Brooke Davenport to bed. Hell, he hadn't even planned to take her home. He'd gone to that idiotic fund-raiser only to get a look at her, maybe talk to her a little, size her up before he launched his legal attack.

In fact, if there had been a trap that night, he hadn't set it—he had fallen into it. The trap of her soft blue eyes, her quiet dignity after that stupid Westover's defection. The undiluted female need that emanated from her lovely body. Her clinging sweetness, the yearning invitation that no healthy, normal male could have mistaken. Or resisted...

No, Charlie would never believe it. Taylor hardly believed it himself.

"But anyhow," Charlie said, clearly winding up to a big finish, "I guess what I'm really trying to tell you is that I'm not going into the custody hearings brandishing any accusations of immorality. If you want to shoot that particular bullet, you're going to have to get yourself another lawyer."

Taylor didn't answer for a moment, lying quietly as Mindy busied herself adjusting the towel, preparing to work on his legs. What a lather Charlie was getting himself into! His agitation was especially strange, considering that Taylor had never once specifically said that he was going to bring Brooke's behavior into the case at all.

He hadn't had to. All the squawking on the subject had come from Brooke's camp. Her lawyers knew what a fatal mistake she had made, and they lost no time in trying to repair the damage. At this very moment, they had an investigator working full-time in the Berkshires, trying to dredge up enough dirt on Taylor to level the playing field.

Still, in the ten years that Charlie had been representing him, this was the first time he had ever threatened to abandon a case. What was it about Brooke Davenport, Taylor wondered, that made men do such crazy, dramatic things?

"Don't worry," he said finally. "It's not going to come to that."

"It's not?" Charlie was standing now, clearly too worked up to sit. He crossed the luxurious hotel room and stood beside the massage table. "Why not? It doesn't look as if she's going to cooperate. You told me to give her a week to get back to you before I filed anything, remember?"

Taylor nodded. "Of course I remember. The week's not up until tomorrow."

Charlie punched the table with his forefinger. "Well, we're going to have to do something pretty soon. It's after 10:00 p.m., and I don't think she's going to come walking through that door right now, bypassing all her lawyers, ready for a nice long midnight negotiation with a naked man in his hotel room."

But at that very moment, a loud knocking sound filled the room. Mindy's hands froze comically around Taylor's thigh. Charlie stared at the door as if he'd just summoned a ghost.

Taylor began to laugh.

"Don't be so sure, Charlie," he said. "Don't be so sure."

CHAPTER FIVE

AT FIRST she could hardly bring herself to knock. But, after standing in the hall several seconds trying to work up the courage, she raised her hand and forced it into a fist. The resulting knock sounded like an angry demand for entry. She followed it with a more restrained tap as if to compensate for the rudeness of the first one.

To her surprise, a total stranger answered the door, a boyish man, in his mid-thirties perhaps, with thinning brown hair and the innocent, chocolate-colored eyes of a sheepdog. She wondered if she'd awakened him. He looked a little dazed.

"I'm sorry," she said. "I hope I'm not at the wrong room. I'm looking for Taylor Pryce."

"Oh, no," he said, rubbing his cheek with his hand. "It's not the wrong room. It's just that we weren't expecting you." He frowned. "I mean, *I* wasn't expecting you."

She nodded politely, trying to follow. "Is this a bad time? I know it's a little late to be dropping by, but it's rather impor—"

"For heaven's sake, Charlie." A new voice called out from inside the room, and her stomach tightened. It was Taylor's voice. "Let the lady in."

For a split second, she thought the man at the door was going to refuse. The door swayed an inch or two toward her, as if he was tempted to shut it in her face. But it must have been her imagination, because in the next second he was swinging the door fully open and smiling her in.

"Hello, Brooke." Taylor's voice came from somewhere in the depths of the huge room.

Brooke stopped, stunned. Though she had traveled a good bit, nothing in her experience had ever included such luxury as this. The sitting room alone was the size of four or five normal hotel rooms. An entertainment center dominated one wall, with two big-screen televisions, both on and set to news channels, though the sound was muted. On the far wall, huge glass doors led to a balcony that overlooked the river.

Even more intimidating, when she finally found the source of Taylor's voice, he seemed to be lying, nearly naked, on a massage table. A gorgeous Nordic blonde, who looked as if she had stopped here on her way to the triathlon, was bending over him, slowly snaking her hands up his bare thigh. *All* the way up, until her fingers disappeared under the skimpy towel that covered the tight curve of his rear.

Something warm crawled through Brooke's veins, and she found that she couldn't look away. His whole body gleamed as if it had been oiled.

"Apparently this is *not* a good time," she said through her dry throat. "I should have called first."

Taylor raised himself onto his elbows, and Brooke glimpsed the golden expanse of his chest, bisected by a narrow, tapering triangle of crisp, dark hair. She closed her fingers around the strap of her shoulder bag and took a deep breath. This was ridiculous. Surely the man didn't receive all his visitors half-naked. Well, if he hoped she'd be disconcerted, he was quite mistaken. She'd seen naked men before, for God's sake. She was a nurse.

She went through the body parts clinically, trying to restore her composure by reducing him to an anatomy prop. *Trapezius, deltoid, pectoralis major, latissimus dorsi*...

"Nonsense, no need to call. I was hoping you'd come." Taylor nodded toward the man who had answered the door. "This is Charlie McAllister, my lawyer."

Charlie smiled soberly, as if he disapproved of something. Brooke wondered whether *she* was what he disapproved of. Her coming to Taylor's hotel room alone, especially after what had happened between them the other night, must seem strange.

"And this is Mindy, who is, I believe, finally finished torturing me for the night." Taylor rotated slightly to slant a questioning glance Mindy's way. Brooke's gaze flickered as the towel lifted briefly. *Ilium*, she thought, *gluteus medius, sartorius*...

"We can stop if you like," the blonde said in a husky voice, dragging her hand slowly across Taylor's leg, apparently checking for lingering tension. "Though I ought to spend a few more minutes on those shoulders."

Taylor shook his head, and with a movement so swift and graceful it all seemed to happen at once, he swung his legs over the table and pulled the towel around his hips, tucking the ends together at the side.

"I'm fine," he said. Standing, he tossed a grin toward the other man. "Why don't you see what you can do about Charlie? He's been tragically uptight all evening."

"No thanks," Charlie said, and Brooke could tell he spoke the words through gritted teeth.

Laughing, Taylor turned toward Brooke again. "I need to grab a quick shower," he said, rubbing at the oil that glistened on his torso. "You don't mind waiting?"

She shook her head, unable to speak. Suddenly, she couldn't remember anything from any anatomy class she had ever taken. The body that stood before her, tall and golden and rippling with good health, wasn't merely a prop, a collection of skeletal and muscular systems. It was, she thought, staring helplessly, more like a visual aid for a class in poetry... or religion. It was potent, beautiful, mysterious... and it was the essence of whatever it meant to be male.

"Charlie will take good care of you." Taylor pointed toward the wet bar in the corner. "He'll fix you a drink."

"No, I won't," Charlie said mutinously. Then, recovering himself, he turned toward Brooke with a stiff smile. "I'm sure you're driving, aren't you, Miss Davenport? You wouldn't want to be drinking and driving."

Taylor chuckled and shook his head despairingly. "You'll have to excuse Charlie," he said as he made his way around the table toward the bedroom. "He's just joined the Temperance League."

The next ten minutes were among the most awkward Brooke had ever spent. She and Charlie McAllister stiltedly discussed the unnaturally warm summer, the value of therapeutic massage—everything, in fact, except the one thing that was on both their minds: the custody of Justin. Finally, they gave up and stared uncomfortably toward the television, where a well-dressed man mouthed something about the stock market.

When Taylor finally returned, they both stood up eagerly, which made him smile. Brooke wondered how he had managed to achieve such a polished look so quickly. He wore casual beige trousers, a tartan green T-shirt and a navy blazer. His dark brown hair was wet, and a couple of waves tumbled toward his broad forehead. He was, she thought, just as sexy dressed as he had been in his towel.

She suddenly realized that, while her attention had been wandering, Taylor had dismissed Charlie, ignoring the lawyer's repeated objections.

"If she had wanted to negotiate with you, she would have telephoned during business hours," Taylor was saying. He glanced at Brooke. "Isn't that right?"

She nodded. "If you don't mind," she said stiffly, "perhaps Taylor and I should talk alone."

"You heard the lady. Goodbye, Charlie." Taylor walked over to the bar. "Now let's see. I have Perrier.

Or, if we can get rid of Dudley Doright over there... I also have some excellent champagne...."

Charlie's eyes darkened. "My room is right next door, Miss Davenport," he said with a quiet, strangely solid dignity. "If either of you should need me."

Brooke was shocked and indescribably touched. She hadn't imagined that Charlie's reluctance to leave was, even in part, for *her* sake. She had assumed that, like all lawyers, he wanted to hang around to prevent Taylor from admitting anything that might jeopardize his legal position.

Sweet, she thought. But what exactly did Charlie think she would need him for? Did he think that Taylor would try to bully her into giving up Justin? Or could he believe that Taylor might try to take advantage of her? She felt her face growing hot as she realized he wouldn't have to try very hard. Even now that she knew who Taylor Pryce was, even now that she knew he had tricked her, she found him dangerously attractive.

It was far more likely, she thought with a mortified honesty, that she'd need Charlie to save her from *herself*. She could just picture the scene. *Help, Mr. McAllister... my willpower is slipping....*

But before she knew it, the lawyer was gone, and Taylor was standing before her, a tall tumbler of sparkling water in his hand.

"You know," he said, nudging the cool, moist glass into her palm, "Charlie thinks I deliberately liquored you up last Friday night so that I could take you home and have my evil way with you."

Sipping the water, she met his eyes over the rim of the glass, but she didn't answer. What could she say?

He cocked one eyebrow. "Ahhh," he said, drawing out the syllable. "You are of the same opinion, I see."

"Sort of." Her hands were so damp she feared she might drop the water. She set it down carefully on one of the many glass-topped end tables. "Frankly, I think your plan was multifaceted. I think you wanted to find out more about me. I think you wanted to get a look at Justin. But most of all I think you wanted to put me in a compromising position so that, if it became necessary, you could accuse me of being an unfit mother."

She forced herself to stand perfectly still, though her heart galloped in her breast. She had come here to talk frankly, and she wouldn't start off by sugarcoating the truth.

"So... the sex was—" he cocked his head "—a fringe benefit?"

"Secondary," she corrected. She could hardly contend that what had happened between them sexually had been any benefit to *him*.

He narrowed his eyes. "Wow," he murmured. "What a flattering analysis. So, in your estimation, then, I must rank somewhere between pond scum and lint."

"I'm just trying to be honest." She took a deep breath. "Surely you aren't going to contend that you were swept away by your overwhelming desire, are you?"

He shook his head, and his gaze suddenly became unbearably intimate. "No. Actually, I think I was swept away by *yours*."

For a minute, staring into his green eyes, she thought she wouldn't be able to force air into her lungs. She remembered how she had clung to him, how she had melted in his arms like a pitiful, love-starved—oh, God, what a fool she had been! She angled her head away, hoping it would be easier to talk without looking at him.

"I—I don't know what happened to me that night," she said, staring at the stock-market man on TV, who seemed much more likely to understand her. "It might have been the champagne partly, and I was...I hadn't...well, it had been such a long—" She broke off, realizing that these explanations would only humiliate her further. "Listen, I know how it looked. You probably think I bring home a different man every night, but—''

"On the contrary," he interrupted with a slow drawl. "My impression was that it had been a very long time since you'd done anything of the sort."

A rush of heat tingled painfully along her cheek-bones. She couldn't even pretend not to understand what he meant. All that pent-up need must have spoken volumes, all that clinging, desperate longing...

"Sorry," he said dryly, sipping his drink. "Was it un-gentlemanly to mention it?"

Ungentlemanly? That didn't even begin to cover it. She felt like the worst kind of fool, and he knew it. He was enjoying taunting her, and she would have liked to slap his handsome, arrogant face. But she couldn't afford to antagonize him now. Beneath the concealing folds of her skirt, she made fists, digging her nails into her cold, moist palms.

"You're quite free to say whatever you like. I'm fully aware that I've brought this on myself." She sat on the edge of the sofa and folded her trembling hands in her lap, hoping her body language would signal that it was time to get down to business. "At the moment, though," she said as firmly as she could, "we really do have more important things to discuss, don't you think?"

"You mean Justin."

Though his expression didn't change, the way Justin's name sounded on his lips was somehow terrifying. She was glad she was sitting down.

"That's right." She squared her shoulders and looked him in the eye, which wasn't easy. He towered above her, ignoring her hint to sit. "I need to know what you're planning to do."

He looked surprised, as if she had said something particularly dense. "I'm planning to adopt him, of course."

His voice was still bland, at least on the surface, but in the depths something dark and slow made itself heard. Not a threat exactly, but close.

"That's not possible. He's already been adopted. By me."

"Illegally." He didn't even blink, watching her over the rim of his glass as he took another sip. His eyes glittered like hard green ice, the first hint that his easy poise might be a facade. "I already have a private investigator looking for Kristina's brother, who undoubtedly is the bastard who forged my name. We'll find him soon—but even if we don't that signature will never hold up in court, and you know it."

She could feel the blood pounding in her ears. Kristina's brother *had* been terribly eager to unload his unwanted, damaged nephew. Was it possible that he really never had contacted Taylor Pryce?

"Oh, I think the signature will hold up just fine," she said, pushing away the doubts. "You're the only one who contends it's a forgery. Our handwriting expert says it's genuine."

"Ah, yes...the infamous 'paid experts'. The best liars money can buy."

She recoiled slightly. "Perhaps that description fits the experts *you've* hired, but I assure you that *our* analyst is quite reputable."

He smiled unpleasantly. "Oh, quite. But he's the third...no, the fourth you've hired, isn't he? The others were somewhat less certain."

She hesitated, wondering why the mere fact of those three discarded analysts made her suddenly so uncomfortable. Clarke had said it was common to have to hunt for the "right" expert, and she had believed him. But now, looking at it through Taylor's eyes, she saw how suspicious it looked. Perhaps she had been too naive.

"Handwriting analysis is very difficult," she began, hating the tentative quality she heard in her voice. "It's hardly an exact sci—"

"Oh, goddamn it, Brooke!" With an abrupt violence that startled her, he slammed his drink down on the table beside hers. Amber liquid splashed onto the glass surface and pooled there, gleaming like pale oval gemstones. "To hell with the signature!"

She held her breath as he came around the side of the sofa. He stopped, tall and rigid, in front of her. His hands were shoved in his pockets, balled so tightly she could see every knuckle standing out against the creamy fabric.

"This is ridiculous," he said. "We can both hire a dozen experts, and they'll argue about every pen stroke of that damned signature for *years*, until Justin has algebra homework and acne. Is that what you want? Is that what you think is best for him?"

"Of course not," she bit back. "I think it would be best if you left us alone."

For a moment he just stared at her, breathing deeply. The nostrils of his straight, high-bridged nose flared slightly, and his eyes narrowed to slivers of green fire.

"*No*." His voice was hard and flat. "Never."

Never? God, that was a cold word, she thought suddenly, irrelevantly. Cold and—final. She stood slowly.

"Well, I'm not going to just conveniently disappear, either," she said tightly. "Whether you like it or not, Justin is my son."

"*Adopted* son."

"My *son*." She hated him suddenly—really hated him—for insisting on the distinction. "Whatever it says on the papers, in my heart he's my son."

He shrugged as if he could hardly bother to argue such an illogical point. "Even if the judge sympathizes with that somewhat sentimental statement, do you honestly believe that he would toss out an uncle's claim entirely?

Be realistic, Brooke. Surely you read the papers. You know how seriously a blood tie is regarded in custody suits.''

Oh, yes, she knew. She'd spent the past week thinking of nothing else, reading of nothing else. The seemingly endless stories of adopted children reclaimed by birth mothers and fathers, wrenched screaming and confused from their homes, had haunted her dreams.

She didn't answer him. She couldn't. Her arms ached as though Justin had already been torn from them. But he nodded, satisfied, as if her silence was the answer he had expected.

"Right. So the best you can hope for is some kind of patched-together parenting that would be a nightmare for any child." Stepping away, he picked up a thin manila folder from the coffee table. Without comment, he rolled it up and began tapping the palm of his hand with it absently. "You can't really want that."

"Of course not," she said as calmly as she could, wondering nervously if the folder contained a legal offer for a custody compromise. She prayed that it didn't. The very words *joint custody* were horrible to her—she had lived those words, and they did not, could not, make a happy life. "You and I don't even live in the same state, Taylor. We couldn't possibly manage anything like alternate weeks."

"No." He slid his fingers thoughtfully along the rolled folder, looking at her from under lowered lids. "It would undoubtedly be something more drastic—six months in one state, six months in another, perhaps. Summers in the Berkshires, winters in Florida."

Brooke's heart stumbled. Did Taylor know, then, about her childhood, about the summers with a father who had lost interest in her, the winters with a mother who had lost interest in life? Was that his subtle threat? If she fought for Justin, she might well end up putting her little boy through the same hell....

For a hideous moment, Brooke tried to imagine herself living such a life. Bundling Justin onto a plane, knowing it would be months before she saw him again. How would she bear it? She had never even allowed her nursing job to take her away at Justin's bedtime, which was a beloved ritual. One splashing, giggling bath. Two dog-eared Dr. Seuss books whose preposterous rhymes Justin would mouth along with her. Three sloppy kisses, and then a final peekaboo with the blanket while she stood at the door.

Her stomach tightened to painful steel. No. She couldn't bear joint custody. She had to be there. Every night. She was his mother.

And yet she knew that Dr. Seuss and peekaboo would seem ridiculously trivial to a man like Taylor Pryce. She strove to sound businesslike. "Unacceptable. It would be emotionally crippling. How could we possibly justify splitting his life in two?"

"We couldn't. That's my point." He touched her arm with the edge of the folder, and the cardboard was cool and impersonal. "Why contest the suit? The judge will give custody to me eventually, at least half the time. But it will be draining, both emotionally and financially, on all of us, especially on Justin. Why do that? Why make it more difficult than it has to be?"

"*I'm* the one making it difficult?" She wanted to scream at his arrogance, her anger giving her a new spurt of defiant energy. "You're the one who's waltzed in here, causing trouble. And you can abandon these fear tactics—I'm not that easy to intimidate. You don't know any more than I do what the judge will think. Unlike you, he just may consider what's best for Justin."

Taylor scowled as though unpleasantly surprised to see that she still had some fight left in her. He probably was accustomed to browbeating his opposition into submission more easily than this. "And that's *you*, I suppose?"

"You bet it is." She met his gaze, stared straight into his beautiful, cold eyes—so like Justin's, though they held no hint of the little boy's sweetness. "Maybe you should do some research yourself, Taylor. Have you ever encountered the phrase *separation trauma*? It's real, and its effects are devastating. Everything from bed-wetting to a lifelong inability to form permanent relationships. Is that what *you* want for Justin?"

"He's only two. He'll be all right." But suddenly, breaking their angry standoff, Taylor moved away from her, prowling to the picture windows. He stood with his back to her, staring out at the artificial starlight of the downtown skyline. Body language at its most eloquent, she thought, suddenly fighting tears. He wasn't really listening. He didn't care. His mind was already made up. "He'll forget."

"No, he won't. Ask any psychologist. These are critical years."

Taylor didn't answer, didn't move a muscle, standing with his fingertips laced behind his back, still gripping the manila folder. His broad shoulders were square and unyielding, as if he could physically block her words from reaching him.

"Taylor, please. Try to understand what Justin's life has been like," she said, half choking on her angry desperation. He couldn't freeze her out now. She had listened to his case—now it was her turn. "He was so tiny when Jimmy and Kristina died. Only six weeks old. He has no memory of his parents at all, or of the bomb that killed them. He almost died, too, did you know that? But now he doesn't even remember where his scars came from."

Still no answer. Did nothing touch the man?

"I'm the only family he knows," she said, and she heard the trembling pain in her voice. But she heard the determination, too. "I won't let his life be disrupted again. I won't give him over to a total stranger."

"An uncle can hardly be called a stranger—"

"*This* one can. He doesn't know you. He's never even heard of you."

Taylor's hand jerked, an almost imperceptible motion, but the drapery at his elbow shivered slightly. He turned around suddenly, and she was startled by the dark tension in his face.

"Yes, and I have you to thank for that, don't I?" He spoke through clenched teeth. "By keeping his existence a secret from me—and mine from him—for two whole years, you've made yourself nearly indispensible in Justin's life, haven't you?"

She drew her brows together furiously. "I didn't 'keep' anything from you. You signed him away because you didn't want him, didn't want a damaged baby to tie you down." He began to shake his head, clearly ready to deny it again, and she felt herself losing patience with his lies. "Yes! It's true, whether you like to hear it or not. Jimmy told me all about you, about the wild life you led, the women and the—"

"Jimmy told you?" His brows contracted, hard and black above his high-bridged nose.

"Of course. He didn't speak of you often, but what little he said spoke volumes. His bad brother, the disinherited brother, the brother he hadn't spoken to in years. Face it, Taylor. I wasn't the one who kept the news of Justin from you. It was Jimmy. He didn't want you to know. He didn't—"

Though Taylor hadn't uttered a syllable, she knew instantly that she had gone too far. His mouth was a flat, fearsome line, and she could feel his fury rippling toward her in cold, tight waves. She stepped back, her calves bumping into the sofa, and her words died in her throat.

But even as she watched, he reined his face under a stony control, and the fury died. Suddenly, in the emotional void that followed, she felt strangely ashamed, as if repeating Jimmy's words had been an unnecessary cruelty. But why? He didn't care about Jimmy, she argued internally—there had obviously been no love lost between the two brothers, even before Jimmy died.

In the whole year that she had known Jimmy, he had spoken of Taylor only once, late one night when he had been too drunk to make much sense. Until then, she hadn't realized he even *had* a brother. "Big Brother," he had called him with inebriated sarcasm, never mentioning his given name. "My big bad brother, who was such a flaming bastard my father cut him off without a cent. And good riddance, I say. Let his whores be his family."

No—they could hardly have been close. So why did she have this awful feeling that her words had hurt him? She studied him helplessly, scanning the granite features. He didn't look hurt. Far from it. He looked impenetrable, as if nothing in his whole life had ever reached deep enough to cause even the least pinprick of pain.

And besides, hadn't he pushed her to it with his insults, implying that she had deliberately maneuvered to exclude him from Justin's life? Oh, yes, he had taken his gloves off first.

"Oh, to hell with it," he said suddenly, with a profound weariness searing his voice. "This is insane." He ran his hand through his hair and, returning to the sofa, picked up his drink, tossing the remaining inch back in one swallow. With the air of someone making a grim decision, he slapped the folder sharply against his palm. "Enough of this random mudslinging. It's time to get serious."

She stiffened. "Haven't we been being serious?"

"No." He sounded irritated, though at what she couldn't tell. "We've just been dancing around the ring a little, checking each other out, discovering exactly how tough the fight is going to be."

"And now...?"

"Now we know." He smiled grimly. "It's a bare-knuckle, no-holds-barred fight to the finish. Your smears against mine, until Justin will end up believing he's related to the most morally depraved people in the world."

"And so?"

"So it's time to make a deal."

She was lost. And suddenly, as if his weariness were infectious, so tired that she could hardly speak. "I don't know what to suggest," she said in a robot's voice. "Short of splitting Justin in two, I simply don't see how we can both end up with what we want."

"The Solomon solution?" The thin smile gone, he held up the folder. "No, I suspect that you'll find even this rather dramatic plan more palatable than that."

"A plan?" Whatever it was, it obviously didn't please Taylor much. He sounded like a man pushed to a bitter, unpalatable extremity. Oh, God, what was it? Her earlier defiance seemed a faraway memory. She felt limp, exhausted, as if she might at any moment sink onto the couch and begin to cry.

Please, not that, she thought. Not in front of him. After the other night, she had so little dignity left.

Somehow she found her voice. "What plan?"

"An alliance," he said coolly. "A partnership for the purpose of forming a family."

She squinted, wondering if fear and exhaustion had scrambled her brain. She couldn't imagine what he was suggesting.

"All the details are here," he said, sliding the folder open to reveal several legal pages of dense type. "McAllister is the only lawyer I know who can make sense on paper, and I couldn't use him for this, so I'm sure it's unnecessarily complicated." He grimaced. "Anyhow, your lawyers can look it over tomorrow. But, for now, it boils down to a fairly simple, if rather Draconian, arrangement. Neither one of us is going to withdraw from this suit, and neither one of us can live with a joint custody arrangement. Still, Justin must have a father and a mother—at least until he's eighteen.'' He tapped the papers. "So I'm suggesting that we take on the job together.''

"Do you mean . . . ?'' She cleared her throat. "Do you mean that we should . . . ?'' Oh, she was lost, so lost. . . . She opened her mouth, but nothing more would come out. The words she wanted to say were too preposterous.

"Yes,'' he said, smiling grimly as if they both had been caught in a cruel but rather amusing joke. "This is a prenuptial agreement. I'm asking you to marry me.''

He handed her the folder, and in a stunned obedience she took it. She looked at the letters, the typed black symbols that marched across the page like precision regiments. The words they formed were only half-comprehensible to her. In fact, the entire concept seemed only half-real. Perhaps this was all just a dream. Perhaps she'd awaken any minute to hear Justin crying in his crib.

And yet the paper felt real in her hands. And the words seemed to take it all so calmly, as if families were created every day out of ink and paper and perfectly organized Roman numerals. She, Brooke Davenport, was here-after to be referred to as "the mother''. Responsibilities, tenure, conditions . . . as Taylor had said, it was all there. Even her "compensation'' was detailed in neat little rows of amazingly large figures.

Compensation, she thought dully. What a strange word that was to find in a proposal of marriage. . . .

He was watching her. "I don't know what to say,'' she said numbly, scanning sentence after sentence, afraid to look up, afraid to meet his eyes, afraid somehow that he'd be able to see deep into her soul, into places that even she had never explored.

Why couldn't she think? Why did her gaze keep getting stuck on that one word? *Compensation . . .* Why did it bury a sting under her heart, a small painful hitch that made breathing difficult?

"I don't know," she repeated stupidly, raising her eyes slowly. "I just don't know. I—I guess I always thought I would marry for love."

His gaze was dark, hooded. "Well, isn't that what we would be doing?"

She stared at him, the papers quivering in her suddenly weakened hands. "Would we?"

"Of course." He raised one arched black brow. "We both love Justin, don't we?"

CHAPTER SIX

IF BROOKE had been superstitious, she would have said all the signs pointed to disaster as, five days later, she and Justin boarded the plane that would carry them to the Berkshires. The afternoon was gloomy with rain, the taxi had been late, and she had a vicious headache from pacing the floor all night, worrying about the wisdom of taking this trip to Taylor's New England home.

Raven's Rest, he had said it was called, built a hundred years ago on the crest of Half Moon Hill. She said the name several times in her mind, trying on the sound, hoping to make it sound less foreign. If she accepted Taylor's deal, it would become *her* home, too. And Justin's.

Taylor had given her one week in which to decide.

He had left Florida three days ago, leaving Charlie McAllister behind to make the travel arrangements. Charlie had been a darling, she thought gratefully. Though she suspected that the sad-eyed lawyer was horrified by Taylor's plans, he never said a disapproving word. He was intensely loyal to his friend, she realized, in spite of everything.

And he was so good with Justin—unlike Taylor, who had stopped by only once, sitting for about fifteen minutes in stilted discomfort watching Justin play in the back gardens, before leaving town. But Charlie had been different, ready in a heartbeat to climb down on the floor to help Justin pound pegs into his workbench.

Funny how fond she had become of him in just a few days. She was immensely relieved when she learned that he lived near Taylor. She'd be glad to see his friendly face, she suspected, when she got to Raven's Rest.

If she got to Raven's Rest.

Unfortunately, Justin seemed to have caught her dismal mood. He had decided to be afraid of the flight attendant, whimpering whenever she approached, and he had adamantly refused to sit in his own seat, even for takeoff. Brooke had to wrestle him into his seat belt and hold him there by throwing her arms across him, which made him wriggle and whimper.

Her bad luck continued unabated. The flight was so turbulent that Justin began to feel sick. He whined incessantly, which caused the elderly woman seated next to them to lecture her companion loudly about this new generation of "spoiled brats".

Finally, though, the woman retreated into her magazine with only an occasional huff. Justin drooped, exhausted by his own temper, and Brooke was left alone with her thoughts.

Which weren't very comforting. Every time she pictured Raven's Rest, her stomach fluttered slightly. It looked like a very intimidating place. Yesterday, when Charlie delivered the airplane tickets, he had brought by an aerial photograph of Taylor's house, as if to prepare her.

She had been stunned. She'd expected a large house, but Raven's Rest was huge, a sprawling, gray-shingled mansion with countless chimneys and gables. Below it, the rich, green-wooded Half Moon Hill sloped away to an eighteen-acre estate complete with trout stream and waterfall.

Beautiful. But could she, who had never even stayed in a hotel half that grand, ever think of it as her home? The stables were bigger than her whole bungalow. Could she, who had never been astride a horse in her life, ever fit into such a life-style?

And the house wasn't the worst of it. What really made her fingers tremble as she lifted her small plastic cup of ginger ale to her lips was something else altogether.

It was the prospect of becoming Mrs. Taylor Pryce.

She could hardly believe she was even considering it. Her lawyers had advised against it—rather vehemently, in fact. Clarke had nearly succumbed to a heart attack on the spot. And yet, once the furor died down, their sharp legal eyes hadn't been able to find anything in Taylor's prenuptial document that wasn't completely fair and generous. More important, they hadn't been able to promise her that she could keep Justin any other way.

So here she was, battling her terror, on her way to New England. The plane lurched over an air pocket, and her heartbeat quickened. Taylor Pryce's wife. Yes, that was terrifying. But something else lurked beneath the fear—something uncomfortable, embarrassing. It was, she admitted, a strange sense of excitement. A thrill that had nothing to do with Justin... and everything to do with the memory of Taylor's hands in her hair, his lips against her skin.

Somewhere along the way, she realized, she had accepted the fact that Taylor was telling the truth. He had not known about Jimmy's baby until about a year ago, and he had been looking for the child ever since. Kristina's brother must have forged the signature, in a hurry to unload the badly burned infant before he got stuck with him. Brooke had been so eager, so willing—the temptation to just shove the adoption through quickly must have been irresistible.

But, if she believed that, it meant that Taylor had been wronged. It meant that her legal rights to Justin were... nearly nonexistent. Taylor's detective was still out looking for Kristina's brother. And when he found him...

She shut her eyes and tried to rest, though the plane bumped relentlessly, as if it were playing leapfrog with the wind. She had to settle her mind, make plans to use her week wisely. She had only seven short days to learn everything she could about Taylor, the way he lived, the people he saw, the food he ate, the activities he enjoyed. What kind of husband he would make.

But there was to be no peace. The next lurch of the plane awakened Justin, and his crying began anew. The woman in the next seat lost her patience, barking a summons to the flight attendant. Justin, of course, wailed as the hapless young woman approached, and nearby passengers joined in the complaint.

By the time they landed in Albany, Brooke was ready to burst into tears herself. She desperately wished she had time to run a brush through her hair before Taylor saw her. She must look a fright. Her rain-soaked clothes had dried in a mass of wrinkles; her shirt was stained where Justin had rubbed his soggy crackers against her shoulder.

Justin himself looked even worse. Weeping had blotched his face, and he had twisted his shirt out of his overalls and unlaced his shoes. She kissed the top of his tousled head, picking cracker crumbs out of the snarled strands as she did so. Sweet Justin. He might be a mess, but he was always completely lovable in her eyes.

Still, she suspected Taylor wouldn't think so. He'd probably take one look at the two of them and decide she really was an unfit mother. She sighed. Perhaps Taylor would be late, and she could dash into the ladies' room to repair the damage.

But of course he was right on time. He stood a head above the rest of the waiting crowd, as elegant as ever in his charcoal business suit. The sight of him, his dark hair gleaming under the bright airport lights, made her breath catch in her throat. When he turned to them, smiling, her stomach swooped down in a rush, as if she were falling from a great height. Oh, God . . . she had forgotten, in these few days away, how handsome he was, how instinctively her body reacted to him.

She pulled herself together tightly. Careful, she cautioned herself. This was how she had ended up in bed with the man after only one dance.

"Hello, Brooke." Sliding the heavy carry-on bag from her shoulder and transferring it to his own, he took in her disheveled state with one quick up-and-down glance. His gaze moved to his nephew. "Hi, Justin. How was the flight?"

Justin buried his head in Brooke's neck, and she heard the low whimper that meant he was frightened. She hurried to answer for him. "It was terribly rocky, actually." She ran her hand nervously through her hair. "I know we must both look disgraceful."

"You look fine." Taylor reached out to tie Justin's sneaker, which was so loose the heel was slipping off. When the little boy sensed the movement, he jerked his foot away roughly.

"No," he said into Brooke's collarbone. "No!"

"Justin!" Brooke was embarrassed, and she rubbed her son's back placatingly. "Mr. Pryce won't hurt you, honey. He was just trying to keep your shoes from falling off your feet."

Taylor's face was impassive as he let his hand fall to his side slowly. She hoped he didn't feel rebuffed. Surely he could tell Justin was just tired and cranky.

"Mr. Pryce won't *hurt* you?" Taylor raised one eyebrow sardonically. "*Mr. Pryce*? How cozy—that certainly has a real family feel to it." He flicked a hard glance toward the cowering child. "No wonder he's afraid of me."

She flushed. "Well, what do you suggest?" She hoisted Justin higher, wishing he would be willing to walk on his own for a bit. He was getting too big for this. "You didn't leave any instructions on the subject with Charlie, and it wasn't mentioned in your documents. Perhaps if you had stayed around a day or two to explain the rules..."

He ignored the dig—ignored Brooke herself, for that matter. He clearly didn't intend to take their argument any further in front of the child.

"What about just Taylor?" He touched the back of Justin's head softly. "How about it, champ? Can you say Taylor?"

Justin burrowed deeper, shaking his head. "No," he said mulishly. "No Taylor."

Brooke groaned inwardly. Justin at his worst—what would Taylor think? Embarrassed, she jiggled the uncooperative weight that pressed against her neck as if she could jostle a polite answer out of the little boy.

But Taylor didn't seem at all fazed by Justin's rudeness.

"Oh, you can't say Taylor? That's too bad." His voice was calmly understanding. "I know how that is. I have a word I can't say, too. I can't say pisghetti."

Justin went completely still, his curiosity obviously aroused. Slowly, he shifted his head so that he could see Taylor out of the corner of his eye.

"Yep, it's just too hard for me." Taylor sighed. "No matter how I try, I just can't say spaghetti."

Finally, Justin sat up. Sniffing back his half-shed tears, he fixed his green eyes unblinkingly on the older man. Brooke held her breath as Justin studied Taylor suspiciously. Her son knew the word *spaghetti* well. It was one of his favorite foods and had been one of his own first words.

"Yes," Justin said finally, frowning, but still curious. His high, clear voice was stern. "You said spaghetti."

"Gee, I wish I could." One corner of Taylor's mouth quirked upward. He leaned forward and made a quick bowknot out of Justin's shoelace. This time, the little boy didn't even flinch. "*Spaghetti* is a great word."

Justin's frown was lightening, and Brooke could feel the tension in his body slowly easing away. He twisted the button on his overalls absently, still staring speculatively at Taylor, sizing him up.

"I like spaghetti," he said finally, apparently abandoning the effort to make sense of Taylor's joke. "I want some."

"*Please*," Brooke reminded him automatically, and he echoed her, though he managed to make the word seem like a demand. Brooke cringed at the spoiled, fussy sound, and wished futilely that Justin was feeling better. She hated for Taylor to see him like this.

But, again, Taylor didn't even seem to notice. He nodded agreeably. "Good. Because you and your mommy are coming to my house for dinner right now. And that's what we're having. Spaghetti."

"Yes!" Justin bounced once, kneeing Brooke in the ribs for leverage. "You said it." He smiled triumphantly, the first smile Brooke had seen on his face all day. He was transformed by the beauty of it. "You said spaghetti!"

"No," Taylor said sadly. "I just can't say that word."

A moment's appraising silence. And then the two of them, uncle and nephew, began to laugh. Just a small chuckle, but it was enough to change everything. The deep voice and the high blended in a spontaneous harmony, the two of them enjoying the foolish joke they had created together. Both sets of green eyes sparkled.

And suddenly, selfishly, Brooke felt a bitter sense of isolation, of being left out of this magical partnership. The intensity of the feeling frightened her. She despised herself for the pettiness of her reaction, but she resented Taylor's easy success.

And though she was deeply shamed by it, she realized that she had liked it much better when Justin had turned away from that unwelcome stranger, the frightening Mr. Pryce.

* * *

It was raining at Raven's Rest, too, but lightly, just soft silver flashes that randomly penetrated the thick canopy of birch and oak as Taylor's car made its way up the hill. It was a long approach, but as the trees cleared, the house appeared in the distance, and Brooke had to bite her lower lip to keep from gasping like a child.

It was the most beautiful house she had ever seen. No, not a house, she thought, surprised. A home. In spite of its size, Raven's Rest projected the warmth and welcome of a fairy-tale cottage. She took it all in quickly—the honeyed light glowing in every window, even high in the curtained dormers; the pewter plumes of smoke that drifted from blue-gray chimneys; the wetly gleaming shingles that made the whole place seem freshly scrubbed.

And the flowers. Charlie's aerial picture hadn't caught the flowers, she thought on an intense, inward surge of pleasure. Even on this cloudy late afternoon, their colors were vibrant, joyful. Rolling waves of pink and white azaleas lapped against the house, covering the first floor up to the windowsills. To the left, in a formal garden, hundreds of roses as red as rubies and as big as her fist glistened with diamonds of rain. Off to the right, a field of annuals spread as far as her eye could see, spilling sweet peas, daisies, flax and forget-me-nots down the slope of the hill.

Taylor didn't seem to notice any of it. But of course it was not new to him, she thought. He took this miracle for granted. While she had sat in a daze of delight, hardly breathing, he had extricated a sleepy Justin from his car seat and brought him around to open her door.

"Mommy," Justin said, waking up and realizing that a strange man was holding him. He began to whimper, bucking against Taylor's chest, trying to wriggle free. "Mommy!"

Brooke held out her arms, and Taylor handed the child over without comment. Justin folded himself against her chest, and Brooke stroked his head softly. He must be intimidated by all this, she thought, her heart pinching. It was completely different from anything he had ever known. She hugged him closer. The familiar feel of his warm, heavy body was comforting to her, too.

Drawing his brows together, Taylor looked away, as if the sight of mother and child displeased him. "We'll leave the bags for now," he said curtly, moving toward the front steps. "Mitch will get them later."

She followed, suddenly nervous now that the moment of arrival had come. She tried not to let her heartbeat accelerate too rapidly. Justin would feel it, she knew, and her fear would be infectious. "Who is Mitch?"

"A little of everything," Taylor replied as they reached the huge double entry doors. The light from the hall chandelier caught in the beveled glass side panels, tossing deep violet and rose rainbows across his hand as he twisted the handle. "The gardener, the handyman, the resident lunatic."

"Lunatic?" She repeated the disturbing word automatically, but Taylor was opening the door, and her attention was immediately diverted by her first glimpse inside Raven's Rest.

It was as charming as the exterior—no pretensions, just a simple, gleaming grace. More flowers, fresh and fragrant; a flowing double staircase that rose, parted, met again at an upper landing; polished wood floors under pale Oriental rugs.

"It's lovely," she said tentatively. She feared sounding too impressed. He might think she was viewing his home through cash-register eyes, ticking up the goodies she might gain from being his wife.

He hardly seemed to hear her. He was leafing through a stack of mail. Apparently whatever he sought wasn't there, because after a cursory perusal he made a small sound of irritation and tossed the envelopes into a nearby silver rose bowl.

When he turned back to her, his face was expressionless.

"What? Oh, yes, it's quite nice, isn't it?" He looked around him, as if trying to view it through her eyes. "I grew up here, you know. I guess I hardly see it anymore."

She hadn't known. And, frankly, she was confused. Hadn't Jimmy said that his brother had been disinherited by their father years ago? If that was true, how had Taylor ended up back in the family estate? There was so much she didn't know about him. But she couldn't ask. Not yet.

"I'm hungry," Justin piped up suddenly, though Brooke had thought he was dozing again. "I want spaghetti."

Taylor pointed through one of the doors that led out of the entryway. "To the kitchen, then, without delay."

Brooke wished she could have moved more slowly through the beautiful, airy rooms, but apparently treating Justin's request as law, Taylor didn't stop for a tour. He led them deeper and deeper into the house until finally they arrived at the kitchen, a huge, bright yellow room paneled in honey wood.

A tiny, white-haired woman stood in front of the stove, stirring a large pot of something that bubbled softly, sending out waves of deliciously scented steam. At the sound of their arrival, she dropped the spoon onto the countertop and held out her arms, exclaiming with delight.

"Taylor, you naughty boy, you've been forever! I was beginning to think you were lost on the mountain. But never mind about that—you're here now, thank heaven!"

Smiling, Taylor bent down for the hug he was clearly accustomed to receiving, and kissed the elderly lady on her pale, powdered cheek.

"I think it's been about twenty years since I got lost on that mountain, Rose," he said dryly, "but I knew you'd worry anyhow. It's your favorite pastime."

"Oh, hush now," she scolded, slapping lightly at his chest, though she clearly enjoyed his teasing. "Stop making fun of a poor old woman and come introduce me to our precious child!"

Wiping her hands on her apron, she hurried over to where Brooke stood, rather overwhelmed, just inside the doorway. While Taylor made the introductions—she was Rose Hodges, he explained, for forty years the housekeeper at Raven's Rest—the elderly lady tutted and clucked, tilting Justin's chin and studying his face. Justin endured this in silence, obviously intimidated by this noisy, tiny whirlwind.

"Oh, and doesn't he just have the Pryce features, too! I'd know him for one of ours any day, the little green-eyed darling!"

Brooke felt her smile freezing on her face. "Our" precious child? Rose Hodges might mean well, but Brooke wasn't ready to let her son become *their* precious child just yet. They'd only been here ten minutes after all. And they might not decide to stay.

"And this must be his beautiful mother!" Rose pressed her thin hand warmly over Brooke's cheek. "Thank you, my dear, for bringing him home to us." Her blue eyes watered. "It's like having Mr. Jimmy back, truly it is. Though it's amazing how much he resembles our Taylor when he was a boy. Beautiful children, the both of them." Taylor murmured a noncommittal syllable, but Rose wasn't listening. "Mitch must come and see him, too. Where is that rascal? He was around here somewhere. Go find him, Taylor, and tell him to come see our precious baby."

"The hell I will," he said, casually irreverent. "God knows what that madman is up to."

Taylor strolled to the stove and dipped the spoon into the simmering pot. With the confidence of one who has been cook's pet for years, he lifted the spoon to his mouth for a taste.

"Rosie, you've outdone yourself," he said appreciatively. "But even so, I'll be damned if I'll go hunting for Mitch. I might catch him stark naked, sacrificing small animals to the moon. And then I'd have to fire him, which would be a hell of an inconvenience."

"I heard that."

Brooke turned at the sound from the back doorway. They all did. To her great surprise, the voice belonged to one of the most gorgeous young men she had ever seen. Barely out of his teens, the newcomer was tall, muscular, black-haired, blue-eyed and sinfully handsome. She blinked. Could this really be Mitch, the lunatic gardener?

He moved into the room and deposited a small sheaf of green herbs in the sink. "I heard that," he repeated huffily, "and I'll have you know that I have never in my entire life sacrificed an animal."

Taylor laughed. "No. Come to think of it, you probably specialize in virgins."

Mitch grunted. He ran some water over his hands and then turned to glare at Taylor. "Your aura is particularly red tonight, Mr. Pryce. A bit overbearing. You'd better watch that, or you might scare off this sweet lady here." He offered a still-damp hand to Brooke. "I'm delighted to meet you, Miss Davenport. You have a lovely green aura."

"Thank you," she said uncertainly, extricating her hand from under Justin with some difficulty and extending it. "Is that good?"

"Very. It means you're quite sensitive. Compassionate." But when their fingers touched, he narrowed his eyes. "A little muddy around the edges, though, and a bit irregular. That indicates worry. Self-doubt, maybe." He cast a suspicious glance toward Taylor. "Mr. Pryce's aura is even stronger than usual tonight. Perhaps his aura is warping yours."

Taylor groaned. "Ironic," he said acidly, "that *you* should mention 'warped'...."

Mitch shot him a wounded look, then bent down to bring his face level with Justin's. "Give me five, buddy," he said, holding out his palm to be slapped. After a brief hesitation, Justin cooperated lustily, apparently pleased to be noticed again. "Let's see, pal...." Mitch tilted his head and squinted. "What color is *your* aura?"

"Aura?" Justin got his tongue around the word, but he frowned, clearly confused.

"Yeah. Your aura. The color tells us about you. You know, like how you're feeling."

Justin's face brightened. He thrust his small forefinger emphatically toward the stove. "My aura," he pronounced, "is hungry."

It was after midnight, but the silent nursery gleamed pearl blue in the light of the full moon, which had finally struggled out from behind the clouds and now floated fat and smiling just beyond the large, arched window. Taylor stood at the foot of the crib, watching his nephew sleep.

He hardly knew how to feel, what to make of the intense emotions that had crisscrossed through him all day like random bolts of lightning, leaving him oddly tired and filled with something that felt like anger.

But anger at whom? At Brooke, perhaps, for letting her desire for a child propel her into a shady adoption that she must have known was unethical at best. Or maybe, less nobly, at Justin himself, for being so spoiled and demanding, so somehow *real*, when it would have been so much easier to handle an obedient doll child, a sugary little cinema angel.

He shifted uncomfortably, resisting the urge to stroke the dark, tousled hair that spiked against the pillow. So strange to think this wiry, clever little tyrant was Jimmy's son. Why the hell hadn't Jimmy taken better care of himself, so he could be here, too? Damn it, he would have liked to tell Jimmy what a brave little devil his son was.

He pinched the bridge of his nose and took a deep breath. So—was that it? Was he really angry with Jimmy for being such a fool, for putting himself and his child in such mortal danger in that godforsaken country? Or— his chest tightened as the unwelcome thought insinuated itself into his psyche—was he perhaps really angry with himself for letting Jimmy die before they could set right their mangled relationship?

Justin sighed in his sleep and rolled over, kicking the covers off his too-thin legs. His nightshirt had hitched up under his arms, exposing the worst of his scars, a long, puckered line of darkened skin that ran from his armpit to his rib cage.

Taylor drew in a sharp breath, recognizing the messy pain that lay beneath a scar like that. A new bolt of protective anguish shot through him, and suddenly his chest ached with an intensity that was almost un-bearable. Jimmy was lost to him forever. But Justin was his now, his to protect. He could never let him go away again.

"Taylor?" Brooke's sleepy whisper came from the far side of the room. "Taylor, is that you?"

He turned, shocked by the sound. He had imagined himself alone with Justin—the nursery had been com-pletely silent, empty except for the beady, staring eyes of the huge stuffed toys that lined the walls. But, as he watched, a tangle of white blankets and moonbeams began to stir along the wide window seat. Brooke propped herself up on one elbow, shoving her long hair out of her face with her free hand.

"Is Justin all right?"

"Yes," he whispered back. "He's fine." He leaned into the crib, pulled Justin's shirt down over the scar and covered him again with the blanket. "I just came in to say good-night."

She stood up slowly and floated over to him, her white nightgown and robe as fluid as moonlight, her face pale and piercingly lovely. She gazed at Justin adoringly and reached in to smooth the boy's hair. Taylor felt another twist of the half-buried anger. *He* had wanted to do that. But *he* hadn't dared, fearing that a strange touch would awaken the boy and frighten him. *He*, thanks to her and whoever had forged his name to those adoption papers, had no rights at all.

Not yet anyway. But by the end of this week . . .

"Why are you sleeping in here?" He wasn't whispering anymore, but he spoke softly. He looked over at the window seat. She had brought in a pillow from the next-door bedroom that had been assigned to her, but had borrowed one of the nursery quilts for a blanket. "That can't make much of a bed."

"Oh, no, it's quite comfortable," she said quickly. "I didn't want to leave him alone, in case he woke up and needed something. He might be frightened."

Taylor's voice hardened. "Why would he be frightened?" He waved his hand across the large, expensively decorated nursery, past the five-foot giraffe who stood by the window, the train that ran along the perimeter of the room, the child-scale red plastic race car with pedals and a real horn. "It's hardly a dungeon."

"Oh, no, it's a wonderful room!" She put her hand on his arm as if to assure him that she hadn't intended to disparage his efforts. "I just meant that he might be confused—he might not remember where he is. He's very . . . sensitive."

"He's spoiled, you mean."

Brooke recoiled slightly, and Taylor almost wished he hadn't said it. He certainly hadn't meant to state it quite so baldly. But there was something about the way she'd been hovering over Justin ever since she arrived—clutching him, white-knuckled, to her breast as if to protect him from the big bad Mr. Pryce—that irritated him beyond endurance. For God's sake, what had she heard about him to make her so nervous? Had Jimmy told her that Taylor ate little baby boys for breakfast?

And besides, it was true. The poor little kid was spoiled rotten.

"I'm sorry you think so," she said, drawing herself up and removing her hand from his arm. "I know he's been a little fussy today, but—"

He raised his eyebrows. "A *little* fussy?"

"All right, a lot." Even in the moonlight, he could see that she flushed. She glanced down at Justin, frowning, as if she feared that he could hear them. "Not here," she whispered. She walked away, toward the far window, and after a brief moment Taylor followed her. "You just don't know what he's been through," she said when they were safely away from the crib. Her eyes were bright, glistening, but she didn't let a single tear fall. "You don't know how difficult his life has been. All the operations, all the pain—"

"I can imagine," he said quietly. He could. He had seen the extent of that scar, and he knew it wasn't the only one. "And I know he's going to have to face even more of that. But he needs to learn to be strong, Brooke. You're teaching him to be weak."

She shook her head violently, but he wouldn't let her interrupt.

"Yes, you are. He's only two years old, and he's already learned how to blackmail you emotionally. For God's sake, he doesn't even walk for himself. You carry him everywhere, like a cripple. I don't think I heard you say no to the kid once all day. I know you do it out of love, but if you keep on this way he'll be an insufferable invalid. He'll be so querulous and demanding that no one will be able to stand him.''

He could tell she was furious. Her chin was high, and her entire body was rigid with resentment. He thought suddenly, stupidly, that she had never been so beautiful. He snorted at himself inwardly, recognizing the cliché, fully aware that she would consider his attitude patronizing.

Yet it was true—and it was far from condescending. He had never admired her more. With her anger and her love both rising in her, she burned like a pure white flame. It was emotion, raw and uncensored. It was also sexy as hell.

"How dare you?" Her voice was thin and icy, but he heard the fire behind it. She clearly wasn't going to take his comments as constructive criticism, and he had to admit he wasn't surprised. "Who do you think you are to waltz into our lives and tell me how to raise my son?"

"You know who I am," he said slowly.

He shouldn't have opened this argument now, in the middle of the night, when she was half-asleep, half-dressed, defenseless. But now that it was begun, he wasn't going to retreat. She was going to have to let him be a real, contributing part of Justin's life. He wasn't going to accept being some kind of powerless figurehead.

"I am his uncle. He is my family, my responsibility, my right. I'm going to raise him, Brooke, with you or without you."

"No." Her lips barely moved. "Not without me."

He shrugged. "That's up to you. You have the prenuptial papers. All you have to do is sign them."

"All I have to do," she repeated dully, "is be your wife...."

She made it sound like a sentence of death, and her tone made him angry all over again. He didn't exactly keep count with notches on his bedpost, but there had been more than a few women through the years who would have jumped at the chance to sign those documents. And why not? He had enough money to be comfortable, a home that most women couldn't wait to get their curtains into.

And he himself, though nothing for the record books, was hardly the Hunchback of Notre Dame.

"As long as we're on the subject," he said, "let's get one other thing straight. I hope I made it clear in the agreement that, if we marry, we'll be sleeping in the same room." He flicked a glance toward the crib. "And I didn't mean *this* room."

She didn't answer. She just looked at him, her lips parted slightly, her eyes wide. For a flashing moment he thought he saw fear in them. The sight bewildered him. As far as he could see, sex was going to be the easiest part of this whole mess. Their attraction the other night had been hot, immediate and indisputably mutual.

And thank heaven for it. He could never have suggested the marriage compromise otherwise. He'd do a lot for his lost brother's child, but he damn sure wouldn't consign himself to a dozen years of celibacy. That saintly he wasn't.

"What's wrong, Brooke?" He bent his head toward hers, so close that his shadow blocked the moonlight, and she was cast instantly in shadows. "We've shared a bed successfully before. Surely it will be no hardship to do so again."

"That night was a mistake," she whispered, but some of the rigidity had already seeped out of her, and she swayed slightly toward him. "You know I had drunk too much champagne."

He ran one finger along her jaw, and immediately felt the tremor that shivered through her skin in response.

"That's true," he said slowly, smiling just a little as he finally recognized the real motive for her terror. How could he have been so dense? Had it really been so long since he'd been involved with anyone this innocent? She was clearly frightened of the intensity of her own sexuality, unsure of her ability to control it, worried that he might try to exploit the vulnerability it implied. He gentled his tone. "But that's no problem. I bought a whole case of the stuff, remember? We'll have a bottle with dinner every night."

She shivered again and, catching his hand in hers, stayed it. "That's nonsense," she said, obviously striving for some emotional distance. "We can't both become drunkards just to make this marriage work."

"No, I suppose not. Well, you have a week to make up your mind. Maybe we should test your theory."

Though she still imprisoned his left hand, he brought up his free one and touched two fingers against the warmth behind her ear. She caught her breath, and her pulse beat quickly under his fingertips.

"See?" He held her gaze, refused to let her look away. "You're perfectly sober tonight, aren't you? Maybe we should find out what happens when we take the champagne out of the equation."

For a minute he thought she was going to cry. The catch in her breath became a hitch, and then a tremble. Her eyes glistened. But she didn't. Instead, she said, "If we take out the champagne, what exactly *is* the equation?"

"The champagne was never the reason you ended up in bed with me, Brooke."

"But what? What is there, Taylor?" she asked again. "There's no love—we hardly know each other. There's no real intimacy. There's no trust. No past. No future. What exactly is this equation made of?"

For answer, he lowered his head slowly. He touched his lips to the base of her throat, an inch above the small, pearl-shaped button that closed the collar of her nightgown. Her flesh was warm there, and as soft as one of the petals from the pinkest rose in the garden.

"It's made of this," he said, his breath raising goose bumps on her skin. His lips glided along the column of her throat, then angled around to the hollow just under her ear. "Or you and me, and the way your blood is throbbing against my lips right now."

She stared at him, wide-eyed, mute, as if she could neither believe nor refute him. As if she were in a trance, unable to sort out the logic of it all anymore. Oh, yes, he thought, feeling the familiar heat seeping into his veins. This was going to be the easy part.

Gently, he put his arms around her and pulled her up against him. She seemed so tiny, trembling against him but not quite resisting. She smelled of roses.

"Relax," he said softly. He traced the shape of her back beneath the folds of her robe—he found the small, graceful angles of her shoulder blades, the gentle flare of her hips, the perfect dip and swell of her buttocks. "Don't fight it."

As if she could hold it up no longer, her head dropped onto his chest. Her breath was fast, laboring, like butterfly wings beating against a strong wind. "Taylor," she whispered urgently, incoherently, "Taylor."

"Yes," he said, slowly massaging the tension out of her, moving his hands rhythmically until gradually he felt her knees soften, her hips adjust, bringing their bodies into a perfect, dizzying connection. "This is the equation, Brooke. It's you and me. Your body and mine."

She groaned, turning her face into his chest, rubbing her face helplessly against the cotton of his shirt. She ran her lips blindly across his nipple and moaned again.

"Your body and mine," he repeated, and he heard that his voice had grown thick, husky, strained. Her lips were driving him mad, though he was sure she didn't know it. "All the answers to every question you ever asked are right here."

She lifted her face then, turning it up to him the way the rose turns toward the sun, and with a deep, groaning relief he kissed her. He wanted this woman so much his whole body hurt. He had wanted her since the first night he saw her.

Cupping his hands around her hips, he pressed her against him, against the painful hardness of him. At the same time, he parted her lips and let his tongue drive once, deeply, into the soft darkness of her mouth. She gasped, but he didn't relent. He wanted her to understand that this time he wasn't going to hold back. This time he wanted it all.

But not here.

Grasping his fading wits, he broke off the kiss and pulled back slowly. She made a small noise in her throat. Looking down at her full, soft mouth and her half-focused eyes glimmering with moonlight, he wondered how he was going to keep from taking her right there in the hall the instant they closed the nursery door behind them. His body burned. Though only next door, his room suddenly seemed much too far away.

"Come," he said roughly, taking her hand in his. "This is no good here."

"Why?" She looked confused, as if she couldn't understand him, couldn't make her mind grapple with words. "Why not?"

How could she have forgotten where they were? He would have smiled at her total disorientation if his senses hadn't been screaming at him to hold her, touch her, take her. To do it now, before this ache devoured him.

"Justin," he said economically. "He might wake up."

"Justin?" She straightened suddenly. He should have known she would understand that name even in her sleep. Her focus sharpened; her hand dropped out of his. She glanced guiltily toward the soundless crib. "Oh, my God," she whispered. "Justin..."

"Come," he said again. "We won't be far. My room is just next door."

But her mood had shifted. The heavy sensual fog was lifting. She was frowning again, and she had folded her arms across her stomach as if to control some agitation there. "I can't," she said in a small, miserable voice.

"It's just on the other side of the nursery. We'll be able to hear him if he stirs."

But he knew, even as he spoke, that it was too late. The radiant, willing woman he had briefly held in his arms had been as ephemeral as a rainbow emerging from a prism. Move the angle of the sun one degree in the wrong direction and the rainbow simply ceases to exist.

"I can't," she said again. She seemed to fumble for the words. "I can't go with you. I can't *be* with you. Not that way."

Thankfully, a leaden weight was replacing the agonizing burn as he willed his blood to cool, his nerves to harden. "Why not?" He watched her as if from a distance.

She wouldn't meet his eyes. "Clarke—my lawyers," she said awkwardly. "They—he—warned me that I mustn't—mustn't jeopardize my legal position." She shivered, then she tightened her arms around her waist. "You know, by having..." A dark, uncomfortable flush crept up her neck, over her cheeks. "By having relations with you while I'm here."

"*Relations?*" He heard himself laughing harshly. "Christ, what a disgusting word. That imbecile Westover *would* use a word like that, wouldn't he?"

She stiffened. "He was just trying to protect my legal pos—"

"The hell he was." If Westover had been here right now, Taylor thought, he would have happily horsewhipped the self-serving bastard. "It was a scare tactic, the emotional equivalent of a chastity belt. Believe me, your *legal* position was hardly the one he was concerned about."

She met his gaze defiantly. "You judge him too harshly," she said, but her voice was strained, as if she couldn't believe the words herself. "He has flaws, but he's a very good lawyer—"

"He's a fool," Taylor said bitterly. He turned to leave the room. This was folly, and frankly it wasn't worth it. She could have her week to make up her mind about this damned marriage if she wanted it. He could wait.

"You don't know him well enough to say that," she said. "He's a good law—"

He whipped around, his blood suddenly running hot again. "I don't give a damn what kind of lawyer he is," he said roughly. "I know him well enough to know he's a fool, and by God I'll tell you why." He grabbed her by the shoulders. Her eyes widened, filling with moonlight and fear. "Clarke Westover is a fool because he believed that what you and I would have done together could ever have been called 'sexual relations'. But believe me, Brooke, it couldn't."

"No?" Her voice trembled.

"No," he said, letting his hands run slowly down her arms. "Never."

He saw her swallow hard. Their kiss had tousled her hair, and a strand tickled at her lips. She didn't ask him the question that hung in the air between them, but he answered it anyway.

"It would have been magic, Brooke. Pure, drowning magic." She stopped breathing, then resumed with a ragged sigh. His voice deepened. "And you know it, don't you? You can feel it waiting, throbbing down low in the pit of your stomach."

She tried to shake her head, but it was a small, weak motion. The trembling had entered her arms. She shivered under his fingers.

"Yes, you can. You felt it the other night, too. You felt it when I touched you." He dropped his voice to a husky whisper. "You lay next to me on your bed, and for the first time in your life, you felt the magic that can exist between a man and a woman.''

"The first..." Her whisper was rough, strained. "No, no, it—"

"Yes, Brooke, it was. I know it was. I watched you, and I know."

She closed her lips and stared at him helplessly. He stroked his hands up her arms again, bunching the filmy sleeves into waves of white silk that foamed around her shoulders.

"I learned all about you that night, Brooke. I know what you need. I know what makes you cry out softly, and I know what makes you scream."

She dragged in a rough breath, but still she didn't say a word.

"And there's more," he said, looking into the depths of her moonlit eyes. "Much more. You know that, don't you? You know there's a place even more frightening, even more wonderful, that I can take you, where the magic will be like a fire, and it will consume you from the inside out. And afterward you will never be the same again."

Her breath turned into a sob, and the lost, anguished sound carried across the still nursery air. Justin, hearing it, whimpered in his sleep.

Taylor looked over at the crib, where the blankets were rustling, undulating, as Justin wriggled up from his deep slumber.

"But by all means protect your 'legal position', Brooke," Taylor said, taking his hands away and stepping back to clear a path to the crib. He ignored her soft moan, her trembling, outstretched hand. "I'm sure Westover will be very proud of you."

CHAPTER SEVEN

THE crib was empty.

Brooke stared into it, knowing there was no reason to panic, but unable to calm her bucking heart anyhow. She touched the rumpled, empty linens. Where on earth, she thought anxiously, could he be?

And then she saw the note, a neat square of eggshell white paper, resting on the soft blue blanket. *We've gone out exploring*, was all it said. It was signed twice, once the bold black word *Taylor*, and once the scribble that she knew meant *Justin*.

Gone? Taylor had dressed Justin—always a noisy, difficult undertaking—and taken him away without ever waking her? She fingered her tousled hair, trying to clear her head. How could this have happened?

Had she really slept so soundly? After Taylor had left her last night, she had been sure she wouldn't close her eyes all night. A heavy, sensual heat had still simmered deep in her core, burning her with every breath she took. She had sat for hours in the window seat, staring out onto the moonlit grounds of Raven's Rest, seeking peace.

But apparently she had slept after all. The ease with which Taylor had been able to spirit Justin away made her feel oddly hollow. *He's mine*, the gesture seemed to say. *I can take him whenever I want.*

Dressing quickly, she hurried downstairs and found Rose scrubbing away at the gleaming kitchen counter. What a whirlwind she was! Brooke would have given anything if Gretchen, who was twice Rose's size, were half the housekeeper.

"Mrs. Hodges," she said without preamble, "have you seen Justin?"

Rose turned with a welcoming smile. "Oh, you're up!" She glanced at her watch. "Taylor said you needed your sleep. I wasn't to disturb you until eleven. You should have seen the two of them, so cute together, whispering and carrying on while the little one was getting dressed, trying not to wake Mommy."

Trying not to wake Mommy? Brooke stared, stunned. Yesterday Justin hadn't even been willing to let Taylor tie his shoe; today they were happy conspirators. And yet, she thought with a trace of bitterness, why should she be surprised? Justin wasn't the only one whose defenses had fallen quickly to Taylor's charm.

"Can't say for sure where they'd be now," Rose continued, oblivious. "Right after breakfast they announced they were going exploring, and I haven't seen them since." She grinned, shaking her head in mock disapproval. "You know how boys are. They'll show up for lunch, hungry as bears and tracking up my kitchen something terrible."

Frustrated, Brooke stared through the kitchen window at the lush, empty lawns. Common sense told her she ought to be happy for Justin—this was just the kind of male bonding she had always known he needed. But for some absurd reason she just felt left out and strangely resentful, as if Taylor had stolen something that wasn't his.

She declined breakfast, insisting that she wasn't hungry, and said she'd wait in the library. But time alone in a strange house dragged, and eventually she began to wander, acquainting herself with the downstairs layout. The dining room, Wedgwood blue with crisp white woodwork and gleaming mahogany furniture. The front parlor, peach, with the windows draped by Irish lace curtains. The recreation room, warm brown, with oak cabinets hiding a state-of-the-art entertainment center.

But, impressive as it all was, time and time again she found herself at a window, peering through the oak branches, trying to glimpse the explorers.

Finally, after what seemed like hours, there was motion—the flash of legs, the swing of arms. But it wasn't Taylor. It was a woman. The legs looked amazingly long in boots and riding breeches, and the head that bobbed among the branches was as fair as sunshine, with a long, shining ponytail that swayed with every step.

The woman opened the door without knocking and came straight in, as if she lived there.

"Taylor?" Her voice was breathy, ultrafeminine, with the modulated tones of the extremely well-bred. "Taylor! Are you here?" A short, listening silence. Then, disappointed, "Rosie? Mitch? Anyone here?"

Brooke fought the childish urge to dart behind the drapes. Whoever this was, she needed to be faced. Within a week, Brooke might be the mistress of Raven's Rest, and it would be ridiculous to start even a temporary reign by bolting from the guests.

She stepped into the foyer, where the young woman stood leafing through the mail that had been piled in the silver rose bowl.

"Hello," Brooke said, trying not to feel suddenly frumpy in her blue jeans and faded-peach tank sweater. The newcomer couldn't help being shockingly beautiful. Her riding habit, which clung to every trim curve, obviously wasn't just an affectation. It looked well-worn. "I think everyone's outside right now," Brooke added apologetically.

The woman swiveled, dropping the mail as if Brooke's voice had frightened her. Immediately, Brooke's own fear abated. Not that the visitor wasn't intimidatingly gorgeous—she *was*, her perfect features finely chiseled as if out of a flawless piece of ivory.

But her eyes...

Her wide-set hazel eyes were the saddest Brooke had ever seen, completely devoid of any sparkle. A faint vertical line between her brows marred the lovely skin as though they were too often drawn together. And the rims were red beneath the thick lashes as if she had been crying. Brooke found herself in the absurd position of feeling sorry for this exquisite creature.

"I'm Brooke Davenport," she said, extending her hand, wondering how much to say. "A friend of Taylor's."

The blonde slowly accepted the offered handshake. She smiled, but in spite of the photo-shoot quality of the smile, none of the sadness left her eyes.

"Hello," she replied softly. Her voice was lackluster, too. "You must be Justin's—" her pause was just long enough "—mother." Again she offered that tragic smile. "I'm Melissa Duke. An old friend of the family."

Brooke's curiosity quickened. That handy phrase often covered interesting truths. An old romance? Perhaps. Melissa Duke was the right age, the right gender and most definitely the right type. Brooke tried to imagine Taylor falling for this woman's delicate beauty, her hint of glamorous tragedy. It was all too easy.

She wondered suddenly whether Taylor would ever tell her about such things. How bizarre it would be, she thought, to marry a man whose past was entirely unknown to her. She might meet daily with women who had loved him, who had spent long nights in his arms, who had been to all those magical places he spoke of....

She took a deep breath. "I'm not really sure where Taylor is at the moment." She flushed as if the admission was embarrassing. But that was ridiculous. Even a wife didn't know her husband's whereabouts every minute of the day. And she was far from a wife yet. "He and Justin went out exploring this morning. They haven't come back yet, though Rose feels sure they'll return for lunch."

"Of course they will," Melissa agreed politely. "No one would miss one of Rosie's lunches." Suddenly, her brow cleared. "Oh, I'll bet I know where they are," she said with a half laugh. "They'll be with the horses, of course."

"With the horses?" Brooke hated to admit she hadn't known Taylor kept horses.

But it must have been obvious. "You haven't seen the horses? I swear, Taylor *lives* for those horses."

Melissa looked surprised, and rather pleased, as if an unspoken question had been answered. Taylor hadn't bothered to tell Brooke about the horses, which were his passion. That meant Brooke wasn't significant, posed no threat of permanency. Her sad face lightened slightly.

"Well, anyway, if that's where they are, I'll be very glad. I was just going down there. I keep my own mare stabled here at Raven's Rest, too, you know."

Naturally, Brooke had not known. Furthermore, she doubted that Melissa's horse was really her reason for visiting today. If so, why would she be here in the foyer, snooping into other people's mail?

The blonde checked her ponytail in the mirror, twisting it around a slim, unpolished forefinger to smooth its curling tip. Brooke couldn't help marveling at how long her thick, wavy hair was, though she had the uncomfortable feeling that Melissa had intended just such a reaction.

Catching a glimpse in the mirror of her own mousy brown mane, hanging straight and thick to her shoulders as always, Brooke felt annoyingly inadequate. But she met her own gaze bracingly. At least her eyes weren't tragic, dull and red-rimmed as if she had spent her life weeping.

Small comfort. *Admit it*, she ordered herself. *You're jealous*.

"Yes, this will work nicely," Melissa said, checking herself in the mirror one last time. "I need to see

Marigold, and of course I'm quite eager to see Taylor's nephew, too.''

Of course, Brooke thought acidly. Finally, the truth.

Melissa moved toward the door, her boots clicking lightly on the marble foyer floor. Hand on the knob, she turned. ''It was nice to meet you, Brooke. Perhaps we'll meet again before you have to go back home.''

Before she went home? Brooke flushed. The sooner the better, Melissa's tone had clearly implied.

Suddenly, out of nowhere, her pride rebelled. She was fed up with being left behind, sick of being reminded that she was the outsider here. Well, when it came to Justin, she was the ultimate insider. She was the *mother*, and the rest of them would do well to remember that.

''If you want to meet Justin,'' she said, smiling brightly, ''perhaps I'd better come with you. My son is still a little nervous around strangers.''

It was a long walk to the stables, and Melissa led the way as if she took it for granted that Brooke did not know the path. Brooke had an uninterrupted view of the silken ponytail, which seemed to sway in deliberate, sensual counterpoint to Melissa's hips.

However, Melissa was so friendly, chatting about Marigold and how the mare was due to foal any day now, that Brooke began to repent her earlier bad temper. She ordered herself to stop imagining the woman in Taylor's arms. It was paranoia—she had no real reason to believe there was any relationship between them.

And it was none of her business.

Yet.

Finally, they reached the stable, a large white building shaded by ancient elms and chestnuts, all in full, frothy green leaf. As they approached, Brooke heard the thundering of a horse's hooves. And above that, a strange sound—a squealing...

It was Justin.

She had to force herself to walk calmly. Her thoughts immediately conjured up the most dreadful images of Justin standing helpless beneath the flying hooves of an angry stallion, Justin falling, Justin afraid... The little boy knew nothing about horses. Nothing! What had possessed Taylor to bring him to this place?

But, listening more closely, she realized the sounds were more like cries of excitement. She tried to listen as Melissa pointed out each of the horses in the stalls that lined the sides of the stable, but her ears kept straining toward the cries. Were they really happy—or was that fear she heard?

Luckily, Melissa didn't seem inclined to dawdle, either. Her tour was superficial, and within minutes they strolled out of the shadows and into the sunlight at the other end of the stable. Brooke's eyes scanned the open paddock, searching for Justin.

Just out of sight, the cantering of hooves could be heard, and Brooke squinted, trying to find the horse. The squeals were growing louder as the hooves beat their way toward the paddock.

Suddenly, from around a curving track outside the enclosure, a huge black stallion rushed toward her, his nostrils wide and flaring. Backing away instinctively, she stared, mesmerized, while her heart beat hugely in her throat.

Taylor sat atop the horse as if it was his natural throne. Erect, graceful, his shoulders squared off against the blue of the sky, his long, muscular thighs gripping the animal's gleaming body. His dark hair was swept away from his brow by the wind, and the reins were looped easily around one long-fingered hand.

But Justin...? Brooke's gaze shifted, and suddenly her head felt light. Her knees jellied. There, nearly five feet in the air, Justin sat, propped against Taylor's strong body. He seemed, horribly, to be connected to nothing. His arms were outstretched toward her, waving wildly, demanding her attention, and he leaned toward her in supreme ignorance of the danger he courted.

"Justin!" She couldn't stifle the anxious cry. He wasn't holding on. She wanted to tell him to grab Taylor's shirt, the pommel, the horse's mane—anything! But she couldn't find the words. Instead, she called his name again, shrilly. "Justin!"

He must have sensed something in her voice, the indefinable something that sounded like danger, like stoves that burn, dogs that bite, cars that zoom out of nowhere. The mother sound.

His face screwed up, and he suddenly began to cry, twisting in his precarious seat to try to get down and come to her. *No, no, Justin, no* ... She took one thoughtless, panicked, jerking step in his direction, forgetting her fear of the horse in a swamping rush of terror for Justin.

The animal reacted more violently than she could have imagined. It whinnied, a high, horrible sound, and tossed back its head. It shied sideways in an awkward, frantic dance as if, unbelievably, it was afraid of *her*.

"Damn it, Brooke! Get away!" Taylor's voice was furious, and she watched helplessly as he fought for control of the bucking beast with one hand—the other, thank God, was wrapped tightly around Justin's chest. The horse backed up as if preparing to rear onto its hind legs, and Taylor yanked deeply on the reins, pulling its head down, forcing it into submission.

Justin ... Her throat closed, screwed shut by terror. The scene before her slipped into slow motion, so that she had time to see Taylor's strong knees squeezing the horse's flanks, his knuckles tightening to bloodless white around the reins, his eyes narrowing to slits of fierce concentration.

Finally, just when she thought she could stand it no longer, it was over. She knew, could feel it in her veins, the minute the horse surrendered. He simply gave in to

Taylor's stronger will, though his hard hooves still stamped the ground with agitated thuds, raising small clouds of dust. Brooke sagged against the stable wall, her throat dry and her heart pounding in the same irregular cadence.

Gradually, she realized that Taylor was making low, crooning noises. The sound calmed her as well as the horse, and the rhythm of both hoof and heart slowed to nearly normal.

"Mommy!" Now that the danger had passed, Justin began to wriggle, desperate to get to her. Taylor somehow managed to hold both child and horse steady. He hoisted Justin shoulder high, smoothly swung his leg over the saddle and miraculously brought the two of them safely to the ground. "I want Mommy!"

Without a word, Taylor set the little boy down. Brooke heard herself gulp with a strange whimper of relief.

"It's okay," Mitch said sweetly, suddenly appearing at her shoulder. She wondered if he had been watching the whole thing. "If you're not used to horses, you wouldn't know."

Brooke threw him a thankful glance, then turned to catch her son, who was hurtling himself at her legs.

"Mommy," he said, bumping his little body against her thigh in an explosive release of inarticulate fear. He grabbed a fistful of jeans and pulled. "Mommy, bad! You scared me."

Brooke understood. Her heart ached for his injured pride, his spoiled adventure. "I'm sorry, honey," she began.

But Taylor strode to them quickly, interrupting her confused apology with a voice like the crack of a whip. "It wasn't your mother's fault, Justin. It was yours. She was worried about you because you didn't hang on to the saddle the way you were supposed to."

Justin rotated his head, angling a defiant look at Taylor. "Yes, I did."

Taylor shook his head. "No, sir, you didn't. And it was very dangerous. If you can't do better than that, I won't take you riding anymore."

Justin's scowl slowly faded as he considered the threat. He clearly knew that Taylor meant what he said. "I'll do better," he said finally, sounding oddly chastened. He hiccuped quietly and wiped his nose on his sleeve. Then he let go of Brooke's jeans and stood up straight. "I promise."

Brooke was stunned—and grudgingly impressed. She had never been able to scold Justin without making his temper flare worse than ever. Not that she ever fussed at him much. It was her job to take pain out of his life, not add to it.

"Good." Taylor squatted, bringing his gaze down to Justin's level. "One more thing, champ. I'd better not hear you talking to your mother that way ever again. You know what I mean?" Justin nodded reluctantly. "Good. Now help Mitch with Midnight. After we put him away, we'll go get some lunch."

Justin toddled away obediently, and Brooke watched him go, a dull resentment blooming in her chest. For a moment she was almost angry with Justin for allowing Taylor to commandeer the role of parent with such apparent ease. Surely respect couldn't be earned in one morning. Love couldn't be sown and reaped in the same day.

But she stifled the unfair thought. It wasn't Justin's fault. He had longed for a daddy—why blame him for accepting too quickly the first man who seemed to fit the role?

Taylor straightened slowly, and Brooke felt his gaze fall on her. He was angry at her for interfering. She could feel it radiating out like cold bands of ice. She lifted her chin, refusing to be cowed. Perhaps she had over-reacted, causing Justin to panic. But she wasn't the only one to blame. If Taylor hadn't smuggled Justin out of the nursery, put him on that ridiculously large horse without her permission, none of this would have happened.

"I don't want him riding," she said flatly, preferring to speak before he could issue some edict of his own. "He's much too young."

"He was fine. He loved it, until you got here." Taylor's brows lowered, though his voice was controlled. "I rode at his age. So did Jimmy. All Pryce men ride."

That was too much. "Check the adoption papers," she said, squeezing her hands behind her back until the blood pounded in her fingertips. "Justin is not a Pryce."

He stiffened as if the thrust had gone deep. But the green ice of his eyes grew even colder.

"I don't think you understand, Brooke," he said with an arctic courtesy. "I don't give a damn if his papers say he's a Tibetan monk."

His voice dropped to a near whisper, but somehow it carried the force of a shout.

"His *blood* says he's a Pryce."

Stimulated by his exciting morning, fascinated by all his new toys, Justin resisted his afternoon nap. It was almost sunset when Brooke finally put him down, hoping against hope that he would sleep through the night.

Alone at last, she wandered out to explore the grounds, which were almost mystical at this time of day. She breathed deeply, taking in the rich scent of the red roses, trying to steady her nerves.

It had been a tough afternoon. As if the scare over the horse hadn't been harrowing enough, Brooke had been forced to watch as Taylor introduced Melissa to Justin, bringing the little boy forth as if he were Taylor's trophy to display.

Justin, bless his heart, hadn't been terribly interested, no matter how lovely Melissa looked, the sun dappling her fair face and illuminating her hair like gold. Mitch had handed Justin a lump of sugar to feed the horse, and he had been eager to use it.

But there had been no lack of interest on Melissa's part. Her smile had frozen on her face, and she'd stared at Justin as if he were the most important child on earth.

"Oh, Taylor," Melissa had breathed, and Brooke could have sworn there were tears in her eyes. "He's beautiful. He looks just like you. You didn't tell me that."

Taylor had shrugged. "There's a lot of Jimmy in him, too," he said wryly. "He's got Jimmy's temper, that's for sure. It'll take a strong hand to keep it under control."

That seemed, somehow, to be the wrong thing to say. Melissa made a small, broken sound and turned her head away. Her profile was a cameo of misery, and in a minute she brought her hand to her lips to hide the trembling.

"Missy," Taylor said gently. He put his hands on her shoulders. "Missy, don't."

"I can't help it," she whispered. "It's so hard. To see him, to see both of you in him, and to know..." She looked over at Brooke with anguish-filled eyes, but quickly looked away as if she couldn't meet her gaze. "To see him and know that—"

"Hey." Taylor had put his lips against Melissa's sunshine hair. "Don't cry."

It had been difficult to watch them, and the memory of Melissa in Taylor's arms had haunted Brooke all afternoon. It had even followed her out here, into the twilight, and for a long time she walked without direction or purpose, remembering. Trying to forget.

Everywhere she went, she encountered more beauty, and she was frightened to realize how easily she could learn to love this place. Above the trees, the sky was a deep blue dome rimmed in sunset pink. The towering oaks cast long purple shadows, and the air was so still that she could hear, far away, the silver spill of the trout stream.

She brushed her hand across the velvety face of a sunflower that grew at the edge of the wildflower garden. It stood as tall as she was, flourishing in this enchanted place. Yes, definitely enchanted. She looked back at the house, and as if by magic the golden porch lights blinked and began to glow.

Her throat tightened. It was like an omen. The rest of the family were all tucked safely inside those sturdy walls, warmed by those shining lights. All, that is, except for her. She was, as always, on the outside looking in.

She squared her shoulders. What rubbish! She was just feeling sorry for herself. She had gone out for a walk, that's all, while the others had stayed inside. Nothing more cosmic than that. She had spent too much of her life sunk in just this kind of self-pity. Since the day Justin entered her life, the feeling had been banished, and she wouldn't let it back in now. Surely the lights could just as easily be interpreted as an invitation, a beacon to show her the way home. . . .

All of a sudden, she came upon the greenhouse, a massive glass structure with an adjoining brick gardener's quarters. She could use another human voice, she thought, to break this mood that had fallen over her. She nudged open the door and poked her head in.

"Mitch?" She called his name softly, not wanting to disturb him if he was busy.

"Brooke!" His voice was pleased. "Over here."

It took her eyes a minute to adjust, but finally she found him, sitting cross-legged in the dirt, wearing nothing but his blue jeans. Slim white tapers had been lit among the greenery around him, and he was bathed in their soft, flickering gleam.

"Oh." She hardly knew what to say. "I've interrupted. I'm sorry."

Mitch hopped to his feet, his lithe body as agile as a teenager's. Which, she reminded herself, he had only barely ceased to be. "No, no! I was just meditating, and I'm all finished." He brushed the dirt from the seat of his pants. "Come on in. I've been hoping to talk to you."

"You have?" She entered his candlelit, flower-filled world carefully, leaving the door ajar behind her and moving slowly between the rows of potting tables. "What about?"

He shoved a tray of seedlings out of his way and propped himself against the table, apparently completely at ease with his half-dressed state. "The biennials," he said matter-of-factly. "It's time to design next year's garden, and I thought you might like to do it."

She hesitated, confused. Of all the conversations she might have expected to have with this young man... "Why me?"

"Well, Taylor told me your gardens at your Florida house were awesome. So I assumed you'd want to plan your own up here, too." He swivelled, rummaging around among a messy pile of papers that lay on the table. "Let's see—I know I had that catalog somewhere in here.... Ah, here it is!" He held up a multicolored brochure triumphantly, shaking little white pellets of vermiculite from its surface. "These guys are the best. Every single seed becomes a flower."

He held the catalog out with a charming grin, and Brooke couldn't think how to avoid taking it.

"I think you may have misunderstood," she said carefully, not sure what Taylor had told him. "I really shouldn't be involved in this. I may not... may not even be here next year." Even as she said it, a lump formed in her throat, and she suddenly realized how much she wanted to be here, to see the seeds turn into flowers....

"Well, of course you will." Mitch smiled happily, stroking the long, thin stem of a nearby miniature orchid. "Anybody seeing Taylor and Justin together today could see that kid belongs here. Man, it was amazing, wasn't it? Their auras were just about an exact match. We're talking harmony here. Major natural rapport."

Brooke pretended to study a little blue flower, though in truth she was blinded by the chaos of her emotions. She would have given anything to deny Mitch's analysis as the ravings of a spaced-out flower child, but she knew he was right. Though she knew nothing about auras, she had felt it, too. The two Pryce males, separated by three decades and one overanxious, jealous woman, somehow really understood each other.

Mitch clearly took it for granted that mother and son were an unbreakable set. If Justin stayed, he reasoned, then naturally Brooke would, too. She blinked as the flower swam in front of her eyes. If only it was that easy.

"It seems a little too early to be sure," she said slowly. "There are a lot of things to consider. It might not work out."

A long silence greeted her comment. When she finally looked up, Mitch was studying her like a puzzle, his eyes squinting, his head tilted at a ninety-degree angle. Suddenly, his smile returned, like the sun coming out from behind a cloud.

"Oh, shucks, of course you'll be here," he repeated blithely, his blue eyes serene again. "You're just feeling a little down right now. It's all that stuff with the horse." Totally at peace with his body and his world, he reached back to scratch his shoulder blade, exposing the dark shadows of his armpit. "And being around Melissa couldn't have helped. Her aura was majorly messed up today, wasn't it? She was sucking off energy from everyone in sight."

He waved his hand toward the candles. "That's how come I was meditating," he explained as if everyone understood about such things. "She left about a ton of energy debris behind, and I needed to clean my chakras big-time. You probably do, too." Standing, he ambled over to Brooke and put one hand on each of her shoulders. "Wow, yeah, your chakras are seriously clogged. I can show you how to clean them, if you want."

"Don't fall for that old line, Brooke," a deep voice broke in suddenly from the doorway. "That's what he tells all the girls."

Taylor. Brooke flinched at the sound, but Mitch, who stood with his back to the door, rolled his eyes comically. He was apparently not at all embarrassed to have been caught barefoot and bare-chested, pawing the boss's lady friend by candlelight.

"Get your hands off her, Mitchell." Taylor lounged against the greenhouse doorway. "Unclog her chakras, indeed," he said dryly. "God, that's awful."

Mitch dropped his hands. "Well, it's true," he said, irritated. "She needs some serious help, and you haven't got any earthly idea what to do."

"Don't I?" Taylor's sardonic gaze met Brooke's, held it like a dare. Oh, yes, he knew, she thought with a sudden melting in the pit of her stomach. He knew. She dropped her gaze to the flowers, unable to face the knowing.

Mitch grinned. "Oh, well, maybe I spoke too soon," he said. "Want to borrow the greenhouse, boss? The candles work great. The plants, too."

"No," Brooke said quickly. "No, really, I'd better go." She put the catalog back on Mitch's pile. "I'd better get back to the house."

"Take the catalog," Mitch urged her. "I promise you it's the right thing."

She looked at him, at his young, innocent face, so eager to indulge in a bit of matchmaking. She begged him with her eyes to leave it alone. "I'll think about it," she said.

"But—"

"She'll *think* about it." Taylor reached out his hand and touched Brooke's back, nudging her toward the doorway. "Right now we need to talk, so you'll just have to trust her chakras to me."

It was a casual comment—yet neither she, nor Mitch, apparently, ever considered disobeying him. His hand on her back was a casual touch, too—and yet Brooke was ashamed of the rays of the heat that radiated out from that spot, as if he held fire in the tips of his fingers.

And as she walked out into the deep violet dusk, with Taylor's shoulder brushing hers, and his hand burning a brand into the sensitive hollow at the bottom of her spine, she shivered. God only knew, she thought, what her aura looked like now.

CHAPTER EIGHT

TAYLOR led her around the back of the house into the kitchen garden, which was enclosed by tall, thick yew hedges. It was almost like entering the center of a maze, cut off from the rest of the world, its air heavy with the tangled aromas of a dozen different herbs and spices.

Brick paths wound around square plots of herbs, and in the far corner, lavender, chives and foxgloves crowded together in a riot of pink and purple. Taylor found a small stone bench hidden in a cutout niche of yew and, with one last nudge against her tingling back, indicated that she should sit.

But he didn't join her. He stood, spotlighted by the last violet shaft of sunset, gazing down at her soberly. He looked very serious, and slightly perplexed as if she were a particularly thorny plant he needed to prune, but he couldn't decide where to start.

Slowly, under that appraising scrutiny, the prickling sensual awareness she had felt began to fade, replaced by an odd embarrassment. She dropped her gaze and fingered the soft blooms of the marjoram nervously. What on earth had she been thinking? Had she actually let herself believe, even for a moment, that he had been planning romance in a fragrant bed of apple mint and rosemary?

If so, she had been a fool. Anything less sensual than Taylor's expression right now would have been difficult to imagine. When, she asked herself harshly, would she ever learn that Taylor *always* had a personal agenda?

"Perhaps this will go better if I start with an apology," he said surprisingly.

She waited warily, wondering what he meant. She wouldn't have thought he was the type for apologies.

"So. I'm sorry," he said matter-of-factly. "I didn't mean to frighten you this afternoon. I had no idea you had a problem with horses. If I'd known, I would have warned you before I took Justin riding."

Warned her, she noticed. Not *asked* her. As apologies went, this one was apparently going to be pretty skimpy.

"I don't have a problem with horses," she corrected politely. "I have a problem with my two-year-old son riding horses."

"Why?"

She shot him an incredulous look. "Because it's dangerous, that's why."

"Not if it's handled properly."

He twisted off a sprig of mint from a nearby pot and twirled it, sending a current of scent swimming on the evening breeze. The smell was startlingly sensual, but of course he wasn't aware of that. He was single-mindedly focused on his own argument.

"If he's with someone who understands horses," he said, "the risk is negligible. There's less danger, actually, than he'd encounter on a skateboard. Or playing football. Or doing a jackknife off the high dive." He obviously saw the shock on her face. "But you don't ever intend to let him do any of those things, either, do you? They scare you because they involve too much risk." A pulse in his jaw beat visibly. "The poor kid'll be lucky if he gets to be on the chess team."

In disgust, he tossed the mint onto the ground. She shifted on the bench, suddenly aware of how uncomfortable it was.

"If you're trying to make me see how necessary his macho uncle Taylor is in his life, you're wasting your time," she said. She stood, too keyed up to sit anymore. "I already know he needs a male in his world. But perhaps, given the physical limitations he may always have, it would be better if his role model didn't scoff at playing chess. That may be all he ever *can* do.''

"Nonsense.'' Taylor dropped onto the bench she had just vacated and looked up at her, his features hard and unsmiling.

She crossed her arms over her chest, suddenly chilled as the breeze, laden now with lavender, brushed past her. She wished she had remained where she was. Perversely, when he had been standing, she had felt at a disadvantage. Now that he was seated, that seemed like the power position, and she towered awkwardly above him, shivering in the night air.

"Nonsense?'' She raised her brows.

"Absolutely.'' He stretched his arm across the back of the bench. "You should have seen him out there on Midnight. He was a natural. The whole thing thrilled him, and his arms had twice the range of motion they ordinarily do.''

She exhaled skeptically. "Faith healing on horseback?''

"Nothing so dramatic. It was just that, for a moment, he had forgotten to be afraid. He had forgotten to feel sorry for himself because he's a tragic little orphan with scars that sometimes hurt.''

Stung, she threw out her hand. "Just wait a minute,'' she said angrily. "He doesn't feel sorry for hims—''

"Yes, he does.'' He grabbed her outstretched fingers and held them in a firm grip, as if the contact could transmit his conviction from his nerve endings to hers. "Listen to me, Brooke, really *listen*. I'm not insulting him. I'm not blaming him. He can't help it. You smother him in pity, and he assumes that's the way it should be.''

"So it's *my* fault?'' To her dismay, her voice broke on a sudden surge of emotion. "Because I hurt for him? For God's sake, don't you? He's only two years old, and he's already coped with civil war and bombs and death. He's endured doctors and hospitals and skin grafts.'' She heard her voice tearing, fracturing into sharp bits on the night air. "Why shouldn't I pity him? How could I not, when—"

His face softened, shadowy in the growing dusk. "Shhh..." he said, and slowly he began to tug at her arm, hand over hand up to her elbow. When she was so close their knees touched, he spoke again, his voice strangely gentle. "It's okay," he said. "He's damn courageous, Brooke. You both are. All I'm asking you is just to let him go a little. Let him see what he's capable of."

Horribly, this kinder tone weakened her in a way his anger and contempt never could. She felt a stinging wetness in her eyes, and her throat burned from the effort to swallow back the sharp, square block of pain that seemed to have lodged there.

"I've tried," she said helplessly, though those weren't the words she had intended to speak. She had sworn never to let this man see how vulnerable she really was, not ever again. "But I can't. I'm too afraid of losing him. I've worried so long, and now I'm not brave enough—"

"Brooke." He tugged her even closer, opening his knees so that her halting steps could lead her in toward him. His hands were on her upper arms now, warming her, melting her icy pride. She felt lost without it. "You don't have to be brave anymore," he said softly. "We're in this together now. But you have to stop shutting me out, Brooke—he's taking his signals from you. Trust me enough to let me in. I can help."

"No." She shook her head and suddenly she was talking very fast, as if she couldn't let him stop her, couldn't let him contradict her. "You don't understand. It's easy, so damn easy, for you to be brave. You don't love him as I do." She shook her head again, anticipating his protest. "No, you don't. You couldn't. You don't *need* him as I do. He's my whole life. He's all I have. I'll never have another child, and you could have a hundred—''

She stopped herself, appalled. Had she gone mad? She couldn't say these things to him, bare the secrets of her private heartache to the man who was her enemy.

''Go ahead,'' he whispered. ''I want to know what happened to you, Brooke. I've been waiting for you to tell me.''

She shook her head in mute confusion, pulling her hands free. She needed to keep her distance, or she would lose herself entirely. He released her without comment, and she moved a few feet away. Immediately, her head began to clear, and the tangy sweetness of the marjoram filled her nostrils.

He was right. She had to tell him. If she really was considering this marriage, it was his right to know.

''I was only sixteen,'' she said quietly. ''My parents had been divorced since I was a little girl. They shuttled me between them for a while, until my father finally just lost interest. My mother wasn't much interested, either, in me or in anything. She never smiled, never went out. Most days she didn't even get dressed. She just lay on the sofa and watched television. It was as if she just didn't care anymore.''

Brooke pressed her hands together, bracing herself to go on. But it wasn't as hard as she had feared. Here, like this, with him just behind her in the darkness, not speaking, but listening intently, it was a little like being in a confessional. Comfortingly anonymous.

She took a deep breath for courage. ''I cared, though. I cared so much it felt like I was coming to pieces, torn up by the wanting.''

''What did you want?'' His voice was gentle on the scented air.

''What anyone wants, I guess. Someone to love me, someone I could love. And then, just when the wanting was the worst, I met Paul.''

"Paul." He said the name slowly. "This Paul...did you love him?"

Did she? It was hard to remember now. She couldn't quite summon up a clear picture of his face—blond hair, blue eyes, thin, tall...but hazy. Too much had disappeared over the years.

But had she loved him? How sad that she wasn't sure. Somewhere high in the trees a night bird trilled, the same three notes, over and over, plaintive and unanswered.

"I don't know that either, really," she said. "It was just that—I had so much love bottled up inside and no one to give it to. So I gave it to him."

"Did he love you?"

She felt a stray tear seep from under her closed lids and she brushed it away quickly. This was an old, old story and it shouldn't hold the power to make her cry anymore.

"He said he did. Maybe he really even did. He was only seventeen, but when we learned I was pregnant, he was ready to do the right thing. He told his parents he was going to marry me."

Taylor inhaled deeply. "And what did his parents say?"

"Everything, all the clichés." She was surprised to hear bitterness in her voice after all these years. "They had such grand plans for him, you see, none of which involved a teenage marriage. They sent him to the minister. To the therapist. To the family-planning clinic. They gave him a book on adoption. They even asked him how he could be sure it was his."

"And then? Were they able to change his mind?"

"I don't know," she said dully, the bitterness evaporating as quickly as it came. "He was in a meeting with the adoption counselor when I began to—when things began to go wrong." Her stomach cramped, the memory so vivid it was cruelly physical. Shuddering, she wrapped her hands around her waist and clung tightly, riding the pain. "I'll never forget it. They said it was an ectopic pregnancy. But that was just a word I didn't understand. All I knew was that I was tearing apart inside."

She swallowed hard, waiting for the spasm to pass. She hadn't ever told anyone this story. Reaching up, she brushed her damp hair away from her face. She lifted her head, grateful for the sweet air that rushed in against her hot forehead.

"Anyhow, the baby never had a chance, not from the very beginning. All the fuss, all the shame, all the hoping, had been for nothing. I was put in the hospital, and Paul was put on a plane to Harvard. I never saw him again."

He didn't speak for a long time. She listened to the whispering sound the wind made through the trees. Now that the story was finished, she felt strangely empty, as if by offering her past to Taylor she had given up a part of herself. She hoped she hadn't been wrong to do it.

"What about the future?" To her relief, his voice held no condemnation, only a quiet question. "What did the doctors say?"

"They said . . ." Brooke watched night shadows float over the garden like dark ghosts. "They said my system was so damaged that it would take a miracle for me to conceive another child." She spoke in a monotone. But it was better than weeping. Better than the storm of grief their words had unleashed back then in that young girl who had so desperately wanted someone to love. "They assured me that miracles do sometimes happen, so I must be a good girl and never give up hope. And then they sent me home."

Finally, she turned around. He hadn't moved from the bench, and in the moonlight she could see his profile. It revealed nothing of his thoughts.

"I know I should have told you this before," she said. "I don't know why I didn't—except that perhaps I was afraid it would give you more ammunition to use against me in court."

He turned his head to face her. A hundred pinprick stars had risen in the black sky above the yew hedge, and his eyes glittered with their reflected light. "Why are you telling me now?"

She shook her head. "I'm not sure. I guess I finally realized that it isn't fair to marry a man who doesn't know the truth. If you had known what...what damaged goods I am, you might never have made your offer."

He lowered his eyelids slowly, shutting out some of the starlight. "Does this mean you're accepting the offer?"

"I don't know," she said slowly. "I think it means I'm...tempted."

"Tempted?" He leaned back, casting his face almost completely in the shadows, rendering it unreadable. "Tempted by what, Brooke?"

"By everything." She swept her glance around the garden. "By all of this. By the life you offer Justin, the support you offer me."

"You mean the money."

"No, it's not the money, exactly," she said, though she knew the distinction was a fine one. "It's what the money can do for Justin. You can afford the best doctors, the finest hospitals. When they decide he needs an operation, you won't have to postpone it while you raise the cash. And even if they can't make him completely well, your money can buy him therapy, security, hope."

She smiled, just a little. "But it's not *only* the money. It's Rose. And Mitch. And the five-foot giraffe. It's the sunflowers in the garden and the spaghetti in the kitchen. You must realize it's a fairly appealing package."

"I hoped it would be." Leaning forward, he touched her arm. Her skin warmed where he grazed her. "Is that all?"

"No," she said, her breath catching in her throat as she met his starry gaze. "You know it isn't."

He let his hand slide down her arm to her fingertips. "Is it tempting enough to make you say yes?"

"Almost," she whispered.

He massaged the palm of her hand with his thumb. "Just almost?"

She shivered as his moving thumb chased golden sparks up her arm. "You have no idea how rare that kind of temptation is for me," she said, and it was true. Her problem was simple and, she had thought, unsolvable: sex was too dangerous. She simply didn't want to risk it. Taylor was the first man who had touched her, *really* touched her, in ten years of frigid loneliness.

She looked at him, at his strong, handsome features, at the intense masculinity that he seemed to take so completely for granted, and suddenly she realized the staggering truth. She was already half in love with this man.

"Almost," she said, her breath short and shallow, "is a thousand miles away from where I started."

He stroked her trembling palm once more, then let it go.

"Any time you feel ready to make the rest of the journey," he said softly, "all you have to do is ask."

The offices of Drs. Portland, Lewis and Thompson, pediatric reconstructive surgeons, were the most impressive Brooke had ever seen—and she'd seen about a thousand, both as a nurse and as the mother of a very sick little boy.

The whole suite was beautiful. Everything, from the wallpaper to the nurses' uniforms, might have been created by some fabulous French designer. The waiting area was huge, hygienically white with cool green accents—not that anyone was allowed to do much waiting. The ratio of staff to patients was about three to one— no skimping on support here—and every employee was warm, intelligent and gracious.

By the time she and Taylor were seated in Dr. Portland's massive private office, Brooke felt more like an honored guest in a luxury hotel than a patient. Silently, she compared this royal treatment with some of the baggage-car bruising she and Justin had suffered in the past months, and marveled at what money could buy. Now if only the medical care was equally impressive...

"Your doctors in Florida were absolutely right," Dr. Portland was saying as he opened Justin's chart and spread it out on his walnut desk. "It's important that Justin have another skin graft as soon as possible. This scar under his arm—" he pointed to a pencil sketch of the human body, with red dots indicating where Justin's injuries were "—is inhibiting his mobility quite a bit. It should be corrected immediately."

Brooke nodded. "Yes. I was..." She faltered, wondering whether she should confess that the operation had been put off while she tried to sell her cottage to raise the money. "We were getting ready for that procedure when we decided to leave Florida."

If he thought her explanation was faulty—and he must know that forty-eight hours was long enough to "get ready" for such an operation—he didn't show it. He just nodded and moved his pen, pointing to another red dot, this one behind Justin's left knee.

"Good," he said. "Now we also think that this one, here behind his knee, is a problem. The skin has contracted so much that even normal movement is painful."

She frowned. "Justin has never mentioned pain behind his leg," she said, confused. "The doctors back home never seemed to think it was much of a problem."

Dr. Portland smiled, generously excusing the doctors back home.

"Well, the contraction is small yet, hard to detect. We'll get our physical therapist in for more extensive analysis, but I did a few preliminary tests, and it's clear to me that he's already compensating."

"Compensating?" Taylor sounded gruff. He obviously wanted more straightforward terminology.

Brooke, who had heard the word all too often, knew well what it meant and hastened to explain. Words provided a safe distance, and they postponed the moment when she had to really think about what the doctor had said.

"It means he's adjusting his movements to avoid discomfort. The way you might walk differently if your shoes hurt. The problem is that compensating can cause permanent changes if it goes on too long, especially at this age."

Dr. Portland nodded approvingly. "Exactly. In this case, with Justin in such an important phase of his gross motor development, if it's not corrected soon, I'm afraid he may develop a hitch in his stride that could stay with him his whole life."

"A hitch?" Brooke's lips felt dry. "Do you mean . . . a permanent limp?"

Dr. Portland nodded. "Perhaps. He would always be able to walk, I suspect, but it might look . . . odd. And the more energetic activities—sports, for instance—might not be possible. This kind of thing is especially hard with a child so young. So much growing left for him to do, and of course scar tissue doesn't expand as well as normal skin. Eventually, the pain would be quite bad."

She felt the blood leave her face. She looked at Taylor. "I can't believe my doctors didn't tell me how important this could be." Her voice was filled with equal parts of anger and fear. "How could they have downplayed something so serious?"

Taylor touched the back of her hand. "It doesn't matter," he said calmly. "Don't let it upset you. Looking back will just slow us down."

Dr. Portland smiled. "Absolutely right," he said. "None of this should be distressing news. I checked out his other grafts, and your doctors did a marvelous job with them. The tissue is quite healthy. Everything took beautifully. No complaints at all, though of course at some point we might want to revisit them, see if we can't smooth things out a little."

He shuffled the papers, pulling a new chart on top. "Right now, we just have to move on, get rid of some of this excess scar tissue that's holding him back. Let's tackle that spot behind the knee first. If we do that right away, I think we can promise you he'll be up and running—literally—in a matter of months. We'll do the arm next. We may have to do some stretching of the donor site, but I'm sure it will be successful." He met Brooke's anxious eyes with a direct, compassionate gaze. "There should be no long-term restriction of mobility, either in the upper or lower body."

"Really?" She had heard promises like this so often— there was no real reason to believe that this doctor was the one who could really make Justin whole again. And yet, somehow, she felt a bubble of hope rising in her breast. "You feel sure?"

"A hundred percent. He'll be lettering in track by the time we're through with him."

"Track? *Really?*" Taylor's amazement was ridiculously exaggerated. He tapped Brooke's hand playfully. "Imagine that, Brooke. Football and skateboards *and* the high dive." He grinned at the doctor. "Brooke had decided Justin was doomed to be president of the chess club."

Dr. Portland narrowed his eyes, but it didn't quite hide the sparkle. "*I* was president of the chess club," he said in a wounded tone. "It is a noble aspiration, Ms. Davenport. But are you sure the Pryce genes carry the adequate intelligence quotient for such an endeavor?"

They all laughed then, with a light-headed sense of relief. Brooke was so happy, so incredibly happy. Though she knew in her heart that the future was uncertain, today she wanted to believe in miracles. She looked at Taylor. He reached out and took her hand, squeezed it as if to say he understood.

Dr. Portland was still shuffling papers. "Lots of red tape to go through," he said, clearing his throat and reverting to his professional manner. "I'd like to schedule the surgery as soon as possible—a few days at most."

Taylor started to pull his hand away, but Brooke caught it with her fingertips, hanging on. He looked quizzically at her, then settled back slowly, sliding his strong, warm palm over hers and holding tight.

"I'll need to start by doing some blood work, urinalysis, the usual." Dr. Portland held up a long, dense form. "So I'm going to need someone to fill out the paperwork. And, while we're on the subject, I think I need some clarification about Justin's guardianship. Mr. Pryce here made the appointment today and says he is the child's uncle. But as I understand it, his legal rights are not yet clearly established." He glanced dispassionately from one to the other. "Is that correct?"

Taylor looked at Brooke. "Well," he said quietly, "is that correct?"

She hesitated. His green eyes, with their soft golden flecks very much in evidence today, were so much like Justin's that she wanted to reach out and touch them, right here, right now. She wanted to run her finger along the swooping black arch of his brow, across the feathered silk of his thick lashes. She wanted to trace those full, serious lips and maybe, just maybe, mold them into a smile.

"Not exactly," she said finally, with a lurching sensation in her stomach as if she were about to step off the edge of a cliff just because someone had promised her she would not fall. "No, that's not exactly correct."

Taylor's hand tightened. Dr. Portland's brows rose. "Oh?"

"Everything's going to change quite a bit in the next couple of days," she said in a voice that hardly sounded like her own. She tried to smile. This was the answer. She finally saw that. The only answer that could make things right for Justin—or for her. "You see," she said, "Taylor and I are going to be married."

CHAPTER NINE

AS MIGHT have been expected, the earthquake of emotion that had tumbled her into that rash decision died down even before they left the medical building. On the way home, Justin babbled incessantly, but Taylor seemed abnormally quiet. In a rush of insecurity, Brooke wondered whether he had already begun to regret his offer. Perhaps he had never really expected her to agree to it.

When they arrived at Raven's Rest, Justin hurried in to see what Rose was cooking. Brooke turned to go, too, finding the moment unbearably awkward, but at the last minute Taylor caught her wrist.

"Brooke." He spoke in a quiet undertone. "Are you sure about this?"

She glanced at him only briefly. "Yes. I'm sure."

"You know that the surgery doesn't depend on it," he went on, his fingers still circling her wrist like a soft manacle. "Dr. Portland understands that I've assumed financial responsibility for Justin's medical bills whether we're married or not."

She felt herself flushing. Did he really believe that she thought of him as some kind of human major medical insurance? Hadn't she told him just last night that she wasn't considering this merely for the money?

She looked down at where their hands were joined. Oh, God... Couldn't he tell what was happening to her? Couldn't he tell she was falling in love with him?

"I know," she replied. "I said I'm sure."

He released her wrist. "Good," was all he said. Then he turned toward the stables, leaving her alone on the front porch, rubbing her wrist where his touch had burned her.

The next few days were difficult, hectic and emotionally unsteady. Taylor, not wasting a moment, immediately set plans in motion for a quick, simple wedding at Raven's Rest on Sunday afternoon, followed by Justin's surgery on Monday.

The details of those two shattering events completely absorbed ninety percent of Brooke's emotional energy. The other ten percent ricocheted like a silver pinball—bouncing from elation to despair, then dropping from excitement to dread, only to be flipped up again helplessly into the flashing thrill of anticipation.

Twice she heard Taylor talking on the telephone, and it was clear he was receiving reports from his private investigator, who was still on the trail of Kristina's brother. Surely, she thought, he would call off the detective now. Surely, now that they were to be married, Taylor would feel no need to track down the forger.

But if he fired the detective, Brooke never heard of it. The whole thing was like an emotional guessing game. Sometimes, in the weak hours of the night, she fantasized about packing her bags and fleeing back home to her safe little cottage in Tampa.

Of course, she never did. Every day, Justin grew more comfortable here, more fond of Rose and Mitch, of his room and the gardens and the horses. Every day, he spent more time with Taylor, less with Brooke. It frightened her, but she tried not to let it show. *Let me in*, Taylor had asked her. *He takes his cues from you.*

Finally, Saturday night arrived. Less than twenty-four hours left... Her nerves were strung so tightly they seemed to hum like live electric wires. Justin was difficult all evening, as if he sensed her turmoil, but somehow she eventually managed to bathe him and get him into bed without a scene.

She had just shut the nursery door behind her with a sigh of relief when she heard the doorbell ring. And ring again. At the third peal, she hurried down the stairs, wondering where Taylor could be. He hadn't told her he was leaving, and he usually came upstairs to kiss Justin good-night.

It was Charlie. The sight of his sad-puppy face made her smile in spite of her tension, and she opened the door wide, welcoming him with genuine pleasure. But was it nine o'clock already? She'd taken longer to settle Justin down than she had realized.

"I'm sorry, Charlie, I lost track of time," she said. They had arranged to meet him at nine to sign the revised prenuptial agreement. "I guess Taylor did, too. He must still be out at the stables."

"What a guy." Charlie sighed. "Here I slave all day over a hot computer, getting these papers revised, and he can't even bother to show up."

Giving Charlie a conciliatory peck on the cheek, she slipped out the door and down the path toward the stables. She hoped it was true that Taylor had simply forgotten the time. She would hate to think that he resented the revisions in the prenuptial documents, which increased the compensation due to her if Taylor should decide to ask for a divorce. Her new lawyer, a short, phlegmatic woman recommended by Charlie, had insisted on the changes, reminding her that if the marriage failed she might have lost years of working time.

It was too much money. It sounded so mercenary. Brooke had argued futilely until, exasperated, Taylor himself had penciled in the adjustment. "It's academic, damn it," he had said irritably. "I'm not going to want a divorce." But still...the whole thing made her miserable, and she'd be glad to have it signed and done with.

The lights were on in the stables, but Taylor was nowhere in sight. She peeked in Midnight's stall, but the horse was all alone, munching on dinner. Black shining eyes stared at her, silently indignant at the interruption.

"Sorry," she whispered. She and the horse had not yet made peace with one another. It still made her stomach tighten to see Justin straddling the animal's broad black back. But she was trying. "My mistake."

Suddenly, from the other end of the stables, she heard voices. Two voices. A man and a woman. The woman was clearly upset.

"Can't you wait a few more days?" Melissa's voice, but more shrill than Brooke remembered. "A week? The investigator is bound to find something by then."

An answering murmur, low and soothing. Two silhouettes emerged from the stall that housed Melissa's mare. The woman clutched the man's sleeve in both hands.

An unexpected fear slammed into Brooke like a fist. She bit back a sound and began automatically to sidle around the edge of the stables into the cover of darkness.

She only half knew why she hid—some mindless instinct drove her. Perhaps she was a coward. Perhaps she was a fool. All she knew was that she didn't want to see this. She couldn't, mustn't hear another word those two shadows spoke tonight, when they thought they were alone.

She made it to the path without being spotted. She walked slowly back to the house, back to Charlie, who sat impatiently at the dining-room table, the papers spread out before him.

"I couldn't find him," she lied. Charlie frowned and opened his mouth to speak, but she gave him an apologetic smile and took the pen from his fingers. "I'll sign now, and then he can sign when he comes back. That will work, won't it?"

"I guess it will." Charlie fixed his big brown eyes on her. "Are you all right?"

"Just tired," she said, grateful for his concern, but dreading the intelligent gaze that might discover too many of her secrets. She signed her name with quick, neat strokes. "There," she said, dropping the pen. "Thank God that's over."

"Brooke—" he began again.

"Charlie," she broke in impulsively, refusing to give herself time to reconsider. "Tell me something. Is there any reason why I shouldn't marry Taylor tomorrow?"

Charlie smiled, though the worry behind his sweet eyes sharpened. "You mean other than that he's an arrogant bastard who doesn't deserve you?"

She touched his hand. "Yes. Other than that. Does he have any—anyone else who might have some kind of... claim on him?"

Charlie was slow to answer. "Oh, I'm sure if you listened carefully, you'd hear a couple of hearts breaking out there tonight," he said, his tone deliberately teasing. "There are a lot of foolish women in this world who for some crazy reason find green eyes irresistible." Charlie tapped the prenuptial agreement, his tone sobering. "But no one who should worry you. It says right here there's to be no extracurricular activity for either of you, remember? It was one provision Taylor insisted on."

"What about Melissa?" She kept her voice neutral, but she watched him carefully. She'd learn more from his face than from his words.

She thought for a moment he was going to pretend that he didn't understand her. He took off his glasses and rubbed the lenses against his sleeve, buying time. Finally, he put them back on and looked up at her.

"Is she what this is all about? Melissa? She's what put that little-lost-kid look on your face?"

Brooke touched her cheek, wondering what had given her away. "I thought..." She stopped. "They seem...she seems... I just don't know how she fits into all this."

Charlie studied her for a long moment, then whistled through his teeth softly. "Well, glory be...I can't believe this." He stared at her as if she'd just grown horns. "You love him, don't you? You really do love him."

She hesitated, then nodded ruefully. "I'm afraid so."

"God." He sighed heavily. "Okay, then. Truth time. Ten years ago, Taylor was engaged to Melissa Duke. He was just out of college. She was a couple of years younger. After a few months, she broke it off—there was someone else she fancied, though that didn't work out, either, poor dumb kid. She made a real hash of the whole thing. But it's over. They're friends now, that's all."

He must have seen the skepticism on Brooke's face. He chewed his lower lip and drummed his fingers, clearly wrestling with himself.

"Listen, Brooke, I'm not saying she wouldn't like to be in your shoes tomorrow. But she's known for ten years that it's never going to happen. She knows Taylor. He's not the forgiving type."

Brooke stood up and went to the window, staring out into the black night. The thick screen of summer trees made it impossible to see whether the lights still burned down at the stables.

She touched the cool glass of the windowpane with her fingertips. "What type is he, Charlie? I know so little about him, really...."

She heard the lawyer scrape his chair back and traverse the room to join her.

"He's the smart type," Charlie said, putting his arm around her shoulder. "Smart enough to know a wonderful woman when he sees one. And lucky. Round about four o'clock tomorrow, he's going to become the luckiest man on the planet."

As befitted a business arrangement, the ceremony itself was brief and dry, just five minutes in the front parlor,

standing before a judge who was an old friend of
Taylor's. Brooke wore the nicest dress she'd brought—
a pale pink sleeveless summer shirtwaist with a sweeping,
calf-length skirt—but it was hardly anyone's idea of a
wedding gown. Ironically, she remembered thinking
when she packed it that the dress would be perfect for
dinner out or a trip to the movies.

To her surprise, Mitch had cut a dozen roses, twelve
subtly different shades of pink, and fashioned them into
a bouquet. He thrust them into her hand at the very last
moment, just as she entered the parlor where Taylor and
the judge were already waiting. He'd forgotten to remove
the thorns, though, and she pricked herself as she took
them, drawing a small, ruby bead of blood. Her eyes
watered, but she smiled and thanked him warmly,
touched by the gesture.

When it was all over, the small throb in her finger was
the only proof she had that anything had even happened. She watched Taylor shaking hands with the judge,
exchanging insults about their relative tennis skills.

Her husband. Was that possible? She didn't feel
married. She pressed the injured finger, perversely relishing the pain. Could something so *little* really have
such huge consequences? Could that nice-looking man
in a gray business suit really say his hocus-pocus and
turn Brooke Davenport into Mrs. Taylor Pryce? Could
a signature on a piece of paper really mean that Justin
now had a father? Could a hundred words and a little
gold band really mean that Brooke would never sleep
alone again?

Rose had fixed an early dinner, and the five of them—
Taylor, Brooke, Mitch, Charlie and Justin—ate it on the
charming brick patio behind the house. Rose had gone
all out, Brooke saw, to create here the festive air that
had been missing from the ceremony. She'd concocted
a feast and loaded a long table with the finest china,

crystal and silver, all glowing pink in the late-afternoon sun.

And she had created a sentimental centerpiece of white roses, at least five dozen lush blooms threaded together with white satin ribbons. It was the only traditional "bridal" detail of the entire day, and slightly embarrassed, Brooke thanked Rose without meeting Taylor's eyes.

Then she tried to forget about the flowers, about the contrast they posed to that prosaic legal bargain that had been struck in the parlor. But she couldn't. Their extravagant, passionate beauty seemed to tease her senses, reminding her of what a wedding could be, what a marriage ought to mean.

Though picked as near buds, the roses seemed to bloom right under her eyes, opening wider as the meal progressed, spreading their petals for the pink caress of the sun, exposing the nubby stamen buried in the heart. Before long, their fragrance was overpowering. Everything she ate and drank tasted slightly of summer roses.

By the time the third bottle of champagne was uncorked, Brooke was having a difficult time following the conversation. She couldn't participate, could hardly imagine herself speaking. Her mind felt drunk with images of ripening roses, her body heavy with its burden of unwanted sensuality.

And Taylor. Always Taylor. Even without looking, she felt his gaze on her. She wondered if he, too, sipped champagne but tasted roses.

"What are you thinking about, Brooke?"

She lifted her head and looked at Mitch, focusing with effort. "I don't know," she said, remembering to smile politely. "Nothing in particular. Why?"

"Your aura," Mitch said excitedly. "It's silver."

"The kid's crazy, you know, Taylor," Charlie put in, his mouth full of salmon. "I've never understood why the hell you keep him around."

"Because he coaxes an extra foot out of every hedge and an extra bud out of every rose, that's why." Taylor tossed Mitch a glance of affectionate exasperation. "And, of course, he's crazy, which means he's always good for a laugh."

Mitch drew himself up indignantly, his blue eyes flashing. "Hey, I know you philistines can't see it, but right now Mrs. Pryce is positively radiating silver light. And if *I* were her husband, I'd want to know about it."

"Well, you're not, my friend, and don't you ever forget it." Taylor refilled Mitch's champagne glass. "But I admit I'm curious. Why is a silver aura such a thrill?"

"Aha," Mitch said smugly. "Because it's a symbol of fertility. It's a great creative power, an open channel of energy. It draws new souls to itself."

Charlie snorted. "New souls? You mean metaphorically, I hope?"

"Not necessarily." Mitch raised his chin and eyebrows haughtily, smug in his superior wisdom. "As a matter of fact, it's usually quite literal. New birth. As in *new birth*." He grinned at Taylor. "See why I thought you'd want to know?"

Suddenly, Brooke could hardly breathe. She tried to move the burning blocks of steel that were her lungs, but she couldn't. New birth... How could Mitch be so unkind? But he didn't know, she reminded herself. Of course he didn't know. How could he? This was just a parlor game, a risqué joke he probably played on all young women....

She looked at Taylor, begging him to save the moment. To make Mitch stop. To make them all just go away.

He rose smoothly. "Fascinating," he said. "Unfortunately, your track record on this stuff isn't very good, is it? You may remember that you told me Rose had once been a love slave to a sultan."

"You told him *what*?" Rose, who had been clearing away the dinner plates, reached out to flick Mitch's ears with the edge of a napkin. He ducked adroitly, defending himself at the top of his lungs.

Covered by the ensuing clamor, Taylor moved to Brooke and held out his hand.

"Come, Mrs. Pryce." He plucked a white rose from the centerpiece and tucked it behind her ear, his fingers soft against her temple. "I hear your channels of energy are open tonight, and I have waited long enough."

As if Mitch's nonsense had decreed it, the room was drenched in silver.

Brooke stared at the four-poster, a man's bed, large enough for two, strong enough to last for generations. Perhaps it had been his father's bed, she thought. Someday it would be Justin's.

But tonight it belonged to them.

The spread was folded back, and there was a blatant invitation in the exposed expanse of glowing star-washed sheets. Loving could be slow here, it promised, with limbs whispering across silk, kisses dragging across skin. Or it could be wild and hard and frantic, hearts pounding and muscles burning....

Her arms trembled, and she crossed them over her belt. She was raving. What did she really know of any of that? Taylor had spoken of magic, but her own wretched experience with sex had been furtive, uncomfortable, rushed and terrifically disappointing. For ten years, no man, not even Clarke, had touched her intimately, nor had she wished them to. Until the fateful night she danced with a green-eyed stranger...

She heard Taylor shut the door behind them now. The slide of the bolt into the lock was as loud as gunfire, and her body flinched in startled response.

"Hey..." Taylor's hands cupped her bare shoulders. They stood in front of the large dresser mirror, and she could see him come up behind her, his body rimmed in silver moonlight. "Easy," he said, his voice low, amused.

But after a second, his hands tightened. "You're shivering." He glanced toward the window, where pale cotton curtains moved in the slight breeze. "Should I shut the window?"

"No," she said. "I'm not cold." But she couldn't stop trembling. Her skin prickled from her scalp to her toes, sending small, rippling tremors out into every part of her body. The woman she saw in the mirror looked like a stranger, her pink dress turned a strange silver gray in the dim light, her eyes wide, luminous with fear.

"What's wrong, Brooke?" He bent his head to her neck. "You're not frightened, are you?"

She nodded slowly. The movement caused his lips to graze along her throat, and a new, cold cascade of goose bumps flooded down her back, her chest, her arms.

"Why?" His lips were at the back of her jaw, and his breath was sweetly warm.

"I'm not sure," she said, tilting her head an inch, two inches...but his lips followed, found her again. "It's been so long...." She shut her eyes, shutting out the strangely erotic sight of their bodies in the mirror. "What if this doesn't work?"

"Doesn't *work*?" She felt his lips curve into a smile. "Let's just say I'd be very—" he kissed the pulse that beat behind her ear "—*very*—" he took the tip of her earlobe between his teeth and nibbled softly "—surprised."

He was so confident, she thought, so sure of himself.

How could she explain to him the terror that had suddenly seized her? She didn't fully understand it herself. She only knew that she had fallen hopelessly in love with him, and somehow love had raised the stakes. What if she disappointed him here? What if, in her ignorance, she failed to make the magic he was obviously accustomed to finding with his lovers...?

It was like betting your life on one roll of the dice.

"Taylor, listen," she said urgently. "You may be disappointed. I know nothing about the kind of lovemaking you described." She opened her eyes and watched him in the mirror. "The other night, at my house...well, you were right. It *was* the first time I ever... And it may have been a fluke. It may never happen again."

He nuzzled her cheek, smiling slightly. "What's the matter? Aren't you spifflicated yet? If you'd like, I can call for more champagne."

She flushed. "Taylor, I'm not joking. I honestly know *nothing*. Sex has been—" she searched for a word "—confused for me. It got all tangled up with pain and betrayal, and... It's been so long, and even then it wasn't...I wasn't..."

He lifted his head from her hair slowly, and met her gaze in the mirror. Starlight seemed to glimmer from the depths of his eyes. "You're serious?"

She nodded.

He watched her silently for a long moment.

"Listen to me carefully," he said in a low, dark voice. "It's going to be different with us. Don't think about what you knew before. In fact, don't think at all." He touched her throbbing temple with his right forefinger. "You don't have to know anything *here*," he said softly. He used his left hand to draw a slow, hot line from her breastbone to her abdomen. His wedding ring flashed, blinding her with its winking silver fire. "When it's right, you'll know it here. In your body."

She shook her head. It couldn't be that easy. The past couldn't really be erased just because he commanded it to be....

But, as if he didn't notice her gesture, he began to slip free the buttons on her bodice. They fell open easily; even her belt surrendered its clasp without demur. Still kissing her neck, he slid the dress from her shoulders and let it fall away. Then, ducking his head, he worked smoothly behind her, easing the way with a trail of kisses, and before she could find the words to protest, her soft white underclothes, so anxiously chosen this morning, had disappeared, too.

She moaned softly at the sight of the naked woman in the mirror. She did have a silver aura, she realized from a great distance. She wore a halo of moonlight, and her whole body was wreathed in a lambent sheen. But her legs were trembling, and she was glad when Taylor rose behind her again and put his arms around her.

"This isn't something you *learn*," he said huskily. "It's something you do because it's right. It's something your body tells you *must* be done." He traced her mouth with both forefingers. "Like laughter." His fingers rose to her eyes, touching the outside corners gently. "Or tears."

He pulled her back against him as if he could absorb the trembling from her skin into his, and she felt the readiness of his body, hard against her softness. Maybe he was right. Maybe he was the magic....

He moved his hands again, and this time he took the swell of her breasts into his palms. His thumbs grazed her nipples lightly, so lightly, and yet their tips darkened and pebbled instantly. She arched, seeking more.

"You see?" He was watching in the mirror. She saw his lids drop over his shining eyes. "Your body doesn't wait to be told. It knows what it needs."

She bit back something that sounded like a sob as he released her breasts.

"Feel what's happening, Brooke," he said as he slid his hands down and covered her belly, splaying his fingers low and wide. "Do you feel the heavy heat dragging at you here?"

She nodded mutely. Yes, she felt it, felt the delicious burning agony of it. It made her afraid again. It was too much, too hot....

"It's just getting started now," he said, massaging his fingers into the sensitive flesh as if he could stir the heat, bring it to a boil. She whimpered and shifted, almost unable to bear it. "It's going to get heavier, hotter, tighter. You'll feel swollen, as if you can't hold it all, as if you'll die if it doesn't stop building inside you...."

Her breath was shallow. Filling her lungs would require more space than her body possessed. "Taylor," she whispered painfully, "no more."

But he didn't seem to hear her. "It will start to spill down your legs," he said. "Your thighs will burn and tremble."

"Yes," she said helplessly. "Please. I need... I need it to stop now...."

"Not yet," he breathed. "It's going to keep building, and tightening, and burning. Until you feel it here." He moved one hand to the shadow of soft curls between her legs. "Do you feel it here, Brooke?"

Yes... She cried out something that didn't really sound like a word, and she began to push against his hand. There, in those shadows, was the answer, the release. He teased at it with his fingers, touching softly—oh, why softly? She craved something rougher, deeper, faster.

And then she felt his hard, thrusting body pushing against her from behind. She moaned, desperate, and tilted her pelvis, angling toward him, her body blindly seeking what it craved.

"That's right," he whispered, his voice hot beside her ear. She took a deep, gulping breath as he tugged her slowly toward the bed. She watched in the mirror as her image receded, unable to speak or move on her own, paralyzed by the terrible, burning need.

The mirror reflected the restrained urgency of his motions as he quickly shed his clothes. Then, his naked body surrounded by a nimbus of moonlight, he sat on the edge of the bed. They both still faced the glass. As if through a trance, she saw the silver outline of her hair, the pearly curve of her breast, the granite glint of his eyes . . .

And then, with one smooth motion, he broke the spell, turning her finally to face him. She gasped softly. The mirror hadn't shown her everything. She hadn't seen the fierce need stamped on his features, the intimidating masculinity of his body, the rippling power of his unclothed muscles.

"Come to me, Brooke," he said, his voice rough and strained. Somehow she sensed what it was costing him to wait. "Let your body tell you what to do."

She hesitated, but suddenly an instinct that knew no fear took over. Slipping her hands beneath his arms for purchase, she knelt, one knee on either side of him, and lowered herself onto him. She let the long, hard length of him slide into her slowly, an inch at a time, allowing her aching body to stretch for him. She groaned at the beautiful pain, a huge, throbbing rightness that threatened to split her in two.

He moaned, too, and wrapped his hands around her waist. "You see how easy it is?" He lifted her once, then pressed her back down. His body seemed to pierce her like a sword, and as tears welled up in her eyes, she understood that she had found what she had been looking for all her life.

Her body knew the rhythm, knew it as well as it knew the rhythm for breathing, and she took him into her, over and over, faster and harder. It was a perfect pain, a magical release, and she couldn't stop, not even when he fell back against the bed, still holding her, bringing her fully on top of him.

Only at the very end did her rhythm stagger, when something inside her seemed to coil and shudder, and she lost control of her muscles in the strangest, sweetest way. He took over then, lifting his hips and pressing hers down with rapid, panting strokes.

And then, just as he uttered a muffled, anguished groan, something inside her seemed to burst. Starlight exploded like the birth of a constellation, and deep within her, a glittering silver flood begin to flow, filling her shattered body and all the empty hollows of her soul.

CHAPTER TEN

IF THE night had been silver, the morning dawned gold.
Fool's gold.

When Brooke awoke and found Taylor gone, at first
she was stunned, disbelieving. Surely he couldn't have
gone far. He would be right back. He would want to be
with her when she awakened on this, the first morning
of their marriage.

All through the wonderful night, he had made love to
her, until neither of them could move. He had brought
her to one miraculous peak after another, proving beyond
doubt that her life of frozen sexual atrophy was over.
Perhaps, she had thought dreamily after one particularly mind-shattering climax, this was what Mitch had
meant. A new birth for *her*, a new beginning as a warm,
normal, sexual woman.

She lay in bed for half an hour, curled naked under
the sheets, hugging her happiness silently to her heart.
Drowsing, she waited for Taylor, secretly hoping that
when he returned he would take her in his arms again,
offering more proof, more silver rivers of joy....

But he didn't come. Eventually, she rose and dressed,
fighting the chill that threatened to settle over her spirits.
She would find him. They would talk. Together they
would go in to see Justin, comfort him, if necessary,
about tomorrow's operation.

She checked the nursery first, playing the odds. But
to her surprise, the only occupant of the room was Mitch,
who sat at Justin's little desk, writing something. He
looked up with a smile.

156

"Hi, there," he said, flourishing the pen and paper at her. "I was just writing you a note." His grin twisted. "Taylor said you might sleep pretty late today."

Flushing, Brooke picked up Justin's blanket and began to refold it. "Ummm...I was a little tired." She tried to sound casual. "Where is Taylor, do you know?"

"Down at the stables," he said, jotting one last line on his sheet and then capping the pen. "He and Justin both went down early this morning. Pretty exciting goings-on. Marigold foaled in the night."

"She did?" Brooke halted, the blanket half-folded. "Did you take care of her by yourself?"

Mitch looked shyly proud. "Well, mostly. The vet came about 4:00 a.m., but it was all pretty much under control by then."

Brooke shook her head. She could hardly believe all that had happened last night. Mitch up till all hours, the vet coming and going, the foal entering the world. New birth... But she hadn't been aware of anything but Taylor.

"Mitch, I didn't know...I didn't hear anything," she said uncomfortably. "We would have come out to help you if we'd known."

"Well, that's as it should be, don't you think?" Mitch grinned. "It was your honeymoon after all. Even Melissa understood that...finally."

"Melissa?" Brooke hugged the blanket to her chest as she felt that first ominous twinge of anxiety.

"Yeah, she huffed around a bit, saying Taylor had promised her that he would help with the foaling. But Rose and I managed to settle her down, and finally she went home." He grimaced. "Of course, she was back at dawn, but I guess that's natural. She did just become a grandmother after all."

"She's here now?"

"Yeah. And she didn't appreciate the grandmother crack, I can tell you that. Her aura just about turned black."

"Is she down there now? With Taylor and Justin?"

"They were all there about half an hour ago when I came upstairs to write this." Mitch abruptly seemed to remember his mission. He jumped up and thrust several pieces of paper into Brooke's suddenly numb hands. She looked at them as if she'd never seen such things before. "Here's the biennial catalog," he said. "And I made a list of what annuals we usually grow nearby. I checked the ones that I know will do well in that spot."

She frowned, still not thinking very quickly. Her mind was locked on the scene in the stables. Taylor, Justin, Melissa... Quite a happy trio. The perfect little family.

"Mitch, I told you the other day that I'm not sure I ought to—"

Mitch looked wounded. "Well, yeah, but that was before you got married, remember? Before you got those silver twinkles in your aura." He squinted his eyes, tilted his head, the way he always did when he was reading an aura. "Still there, by the way. Anyhow, I figured a wedding pretty much settled things, don't you think? No question now of whether you'll *be* here next summer, I guess, huh?"

What could she say? She had signed a prenuptial agreement that specifically listed the circumstances under which she would be justified in terminating this marriage. Physical abuse, mental abuse, nonsupport, sexual neglect, abandonment, adultery...

No. The fact that her new husband was spending the morning after in the stables with Melissa Duke definitely wasn't on that list. Brooke would be here next summer, or she'd be back in court fighting for Justin.

"All right," she said, staring down at the color brochure, hating its cheerful colors, its overblown blossoms and touched-up photos. "I'll work on it."

But somehow she didn't think she really would. She sank onto the window seat, watching as Mitch marched merrily toward the stables. As much as it hurt, she had to be realistic. There were so many ways this artificial marriage could fall apart....

Taylor still had a private detective on the forgery case—how long before the investigator found Kristina's brother, Samuel, who would probably admit to his fraud just to save his own selfish neck? The thought raised goose bumps on her arms. And God alone knew what else the man would say....

Then, when Taylor didn't have to fear losing Justin in a custody battle, how long before he tired of his new wife toy? He'd conquered her now, proved his prowess by overcoming her fears. How long before that triumphant honeymoon glow faded—if indeed it hadn't already?

Or... another grim scenario. How long before an argument over how to handle Justin turned into a rift, a gulf, an alienation? How long before Melissa's broken heart looked romantic, tragic, inviting? How long before mornings in the stables turned into midnights in the hay?

No, she didn't think she'd be making long-term garden plans just yet. She folded the brochure and put it in her skirt pocket. It was a lot easier to picture herself in a courtroom than it was to see herself still at Raven's Rest when summer came again.

In spite of everything, her heart leaped when she heard voices at the door. She put down the magazine she'd been trying to read and smoothed her hair with fingertips that trembled slightly. Taylor...

But it wasn't Taylor. It was Mitch, who had met a newcomer at the door and now showed him in with a scowl.

"Brooke," he said in a monotone that was totally unlike his normal ebullient self. "Someone to see you."

Brooke stood, staring. Though she could hardly believe the evidence of her own eyes, it was Clarke. She blinked as if to clear her vision, but his handsome blond face, which looked extremely out of sorts, was still there in front of her.

"Clarke!" She moved forward, belatedly reaching out one hand to invite him into the room. "What on earth are you doing here?"

He bristled, twitching his shoulders. "Well, that's quite a welcome." He took the proffered hand. "I've come all this way because we got word that you were actually going to marry Taylor Pryce." He glimpsed the simple gold band on her ring finger. "I see it's true."

"Yes." She eased her hand free. "I called your office and told them to let you know. We were married yesterday." She smiled, hoping to soften the blow she knew his pride had taken. "It seemed the best for everyone, Clarke."

"For Pryce, perhaps," Clarke said with a clipped distaste. "And maybe for the child. But not for you." He studied her face. "I know you, Brooke. You don't look happy. You look tired."

"Well, what do you think?" Mitch broke in irritably. "It was her wedding night, for pity's sake. You think she spent it sleeping?"

Brooke shot a quelling look at the young man. He obviously didn't like Clarke, and heaven only knew what he might say. And Clarke didn't look to be in the mood to take any sass from the New Age gardener.

"Mitch," she said gently, "Clarke is an old friend. He used to be my attorney."

Mitch squinted, eyeing Clarke from head to toe. "Yeah? Well, I don't care. He's got a muddy aura, damn it. Something's seriously out of alignment in this dude."

"What the...?" Clarke's face reddened. This was not the kind of treatment he was used to. His hands made fists at his sides. "I'll show you something out of alignment, you head case."

Brooke hurried to Clarke's side. She touched his arm calmingly. "Don't mind Mitch," she said. "He's been up all night foaling a mare, and he's very tired." She turned to face the younger man, whose blue eyes were flashing. "Aren't you tired, Mitch? Probably you just want to go meditate a little while, clean out your chakras, which are clearly all clogged up at the moment." She gave him an intimate smile. "Right?"

Thankfully, he got the message. "Yeah, sure," he said, though he still sounded peeved. "I'll go check on Marigold, and then I'll go light a candle in the greenhouse." He got as far as the doorway, then turned back to glare at Clarke. "While I'm at it, I'll pray for the removal of all negative influences. The departure of all muddy-aura mouth breathers."

Pleased with his parting line, he finally left. But after that insult it took several minutes for Brooke to calm Clarke enough to discuss the point of his visit. What a bore his sensitive ego was! Brooke realized after only a minute or two that she just couldn't bring herself to baby this arrogant man anymore. And, even more freeing, that she didn't have to.

"For God's sake, Clarke, forget about Mitch," she said finally, her voice sharper than usual. "So he doesn't like you. You'll never see him again, so what do you care? Just tell me why you've come."

"Well, I've come with good news," he said, huffy, but bringing forth a packet of papers from his breast pocket anyway. "I've come with an offer from Alston. He's prepared to buy your house. And at a rather generous price, too."

She took the packet reluctantly. "But Clarke, I don't need to sell the house anymore. I thought you'd understand that. Now that we're married, Taylor is taking care of Justin's medical bills."

"Taylor!" Clarke's face grew ruddy again. "Listen, Brooke, you can't back out on this now. You came to me, remember? You begged me to approach Alston for you. Well, I did. And I talked him into making an offer. If I go back now and tell him you've changed your mind, I'll look like a bloody fool."

She stared at the papers, uncertain. On the one hand, Clarke was right. She had begged him to do this. On the other, she had always hated the prospect of selling her grandmother's cottage. Only for Justin would she have contemplated such a sacrifice.

"I'm so sorry, Clarke," she said, handing the papers back to him. That was sincere at least. She *was* sorry to have put him in an awkward situation with such an important client. "But the cottage is very special to me. I just don't want to lose it if I can possibly help it."

Clarke refused to take the document from her hands. His cheeks were as darkly red as wine, and she knew he was furious. "If I were you, I'd give this some more thought, Brooke," he said. "This is a lot of money. And you never know when you might need money in a big hurry."

She let her hand fall, dangling the papers at her side. "What exactly is that supposed to mean?"

He snorted. "It means that this relationship between you and Pryce is, at best, pretty damn fragile. Marriages of convenience often turn out to be maddeningly inconvenient. I've seen it happen a hundred times, Brooke, and I'd hate to see it happen to you. The prenup Taylor offered you is generous, but even a generous settlement isn't going to pay for a dozen more skin grafts."

His words so perfectly echoed her earlier tormented fears that she could hardly think how to answer him. "Nonsense," she said, but it sounded weak. Even she could hear the fear in the word.

"You think so? Well, did you know that your *husband*—" he drawled the word irreverently "—is still looking for Justin's other uncle? You know the one...Kristina's brother, Samuel, the one who can prove that the adoption was illegal?"

She nodded. "Yes," she said, holding her voice steady with effort. "I knew that. But he hired that private detective long ago, before we decided to marry."

"So why is the guy still out there combing Europe, spending thousands of Pryce dollars? God, Brooke, are you really too naive to see what's right in front of your nose? He's still out there because Pryce wants to have all his ammunition ready in case the marriage doesn't work out. If he's protecting himself, why shouldn't you do the same?"

"That's not true." Brooke kept her voice low, for fear it might spiral out of control. "Taylor understands that Justin needs me. We're planning to make a real family, to be real parents—"

"Oh, grow up, Brooke!" Clarke was clearly disgusted. "Do you really believe a man like Pryce is going to play house indefinitely with someone like you? Do you think *he* will go for two years settling for a couple of limp kisses here and there while he tries to thaw you out?" He made a derisive sound in his throat. "Not likely. *I'm* the only one who's fool enough for that."

"Maybe you're right." She tightened her voice. "Maybe Taylor wouldn't wait that long." She smiled thinly. "But then...he didn't have to."

Clarke's sneer froze comically on his face for a long, stunned moment. She watched as he slowly recovered from the shock, reaching deep inside himself for something to say that would avenge his pride.

"So. He's already stormed the gates to the ice palace, has he?" He narrowed his eyes. "Smart man—he's going to have it all. He'll get his kicks with you until he finds the missing uncle, and then he'll be able to off-load you like yesterday's baggage and still keep the kid." He whistled. "Well, damn. *I'm* impressed."

But Brooke had finally had enough. She dropped the real-estate papers on the end table with a small thud.

"Find your own way out, Clarke," she said, her voice staccato and cold. "And don't come back. I never want to see you again."

Taylor didn't come back until lunchtime. Brooke was in the nursery, packing Justin's things. They would be leaving for the hospital right after they ate, and she wanted to be ready. Besides, she found the large, sunny room somehow soothing, with its smiling animals and colorful, tinkling balls. She held his blanket to her face. It smelled comfortingly of Justin.

The time hung heavily in the air, but she fought the urge to go down to the stables, even though she suspected Justin might be missing her. Usually right before an operation, he was tearful, unruly and demanding.

Let Taylor deal with it, she thought, her hurt feelings taking refuge in anger. If he needed her, he knew where she was. She wouldn't go searching for him like the tragic, abandoned wife. She had no reason to feel tragic. She had wanted to provide a safe environment for her son, and she had done so. If Taylor would prefer to spend his spare time with Melissa Duke, that was his business.

She heard their returning clamor several minutes before she saw them. To her amazement, Justin didn't sound weepy at all. He pounded up the stairs and then went streaking by, with his odd little limping run, squealing with delighted terror.

"Hi, Mommy," he called as he flew past, barely pausing to wave.

Rose followed hard on his heels. "You'd better get in that bathtub, young man. You're not going to the hospital smelling like horses if I have anything to say about it."

Brooke turned back to her packing. She focused on Justin's happy face. She assured herself that she was glad

Taylor and Melissa had managed to keep the boy's spirits so high.

After a few minutes, she heard Taylor's footsteps. She knew that he stood in the doorway for several seconds before he spoke.

"Good morning," he said neutrally. "Did you sleep well?"

She glanced at the nursery clock. "Good afternoon," she corrected mildly. "Yes, fine, thanks. And you?"

The formal tone was so strange, she thought numbly. It was as if they were two different people, surely not the same man and woman who had last night discovered such exotic delights among the tangled silver sheets, loving each other's bodies until they were damp with sweat and limp with pleasure...

Taylor entered the room slowly and stopped right behind her. The nape of her neck tingled with awareness, but she didn't turn around.

"Justin and I have been at the stables," he said. "Marigold foaled last night. I thought you might come down."

She fisted her hand in one of Justin's shirts, biting back all the angry words that rose in her throat. "And I," she said tersely, "foolishly thought that you might come here."

He leaned against the changing table and handed her a box of diapers. "I would have," he said coolly, "but Mitch told me you had company."

Her clumsy fingers dropped the box onto the floor. Taylor bent down and retrieved it without a word.

"Yes," she said, furious with herself for feeling so strangely guilty. Why should she? She hadn't asked Clarke to come. She hadn't wanted him here, and she had sent him quickly on his way. How dare Taylor take that cold, accusatory tone? "Clarke came by to talk to me."

"Clarke *came by*?" He repeated the phrase with a low undercurrent of sarcasm. He picked up one of Justin's nightshirts and began to fold it studiously. "He happened to be in the neighborhood, you mean? He's only about a thousand miles from home."

"He flew up this morning. He had an offer on my house," she explained. She looked at Taylor. "I had asked him to sell it for me before—before I came up here. He wanted me to know there was an offer on it in case I still needed the money."

"You don't need money. You don't need anything Clarke Westover has," Taylor said, his words deliberate and clipped, his hands mangling the nightshirt. "Perhaps you'd better tell him that next time. Better still, if there is a next time, why don't you let me tell him?"

His eyes were ice green. He was angry, too, she realized. Very angry. How typically male it was for him to resent Clarke's arrival, completely ignoring the fact that he himself had spent the morning with his *own* ex-fiancée. She could hardly believe his peremptory tone, his domineering assumption that he could dictate how she spent every minute of her life. And with whom.

Where, she thought, were *her* rights? Could she dictate what company *he* kept? She could only imagine what he would say if she told him that she didn't want him spending time with Melissa anymore, that she didn't trust him. . . .

How quickly, she suspected, this makeshift marriage would start to fall apart then.

"Well, perhaps I should be thinking about setting aside more money," she said, lifting her chin. "If this doesn't work out, I will have to take care of myself and Justin again, you know."

"What do you mean, if it doesn't work?" He narrowed his eyes. "I think we proved last night that it works just fine."

"I mean the whole marriage," she said acidly. "It is possible to have successful sex and still have an unsuccessful marriage, you know. There are about a hundred ways this could blow up in our faces, as you so scrupulously detailed in your prenuptial agreement. I'm simply following your lead. I'd be foolish not to protect myself, don't you think?"

"Protect yourself?" He tossed the shirt roughly into the suitcase. "Is that what the wise Mr. Westover was telling you to do?"

"Yes," she said steadily. "As a matter of fact, it was."

"Damn it, Brooke." He grabbed her arm, his fingers hard against her skin. "Since when do you listen to that son of a bitch?"

"Since he began to make sense," she said coldly. "Now please let go. You're hurting me."

For an ugly moment, she was afraid he wouldn't do it. His fingers tightened further, and he began to tug her toward him, his eyes flashing with a strange green-and-gold fire.

But at that moment, Justin came storming in, wearing nothing but a towel slung around his hips, which dragged on the ground behind him. His hair was wet, dripping into his face, but he was smiling broadly.

"Mommy, guess what?" He flung himself toward her, and Taylor stepped back abruptly, clearing the way. "Guess what? Missy says if I'm really good for the doctor, she'll give me the new horse baby."

Brooke's cheeks flamed with anger. If Melissa wanted to flirt with Taylor, they were both adults and could do as they pleased. But when she began making overtures to Justin, trying to insinuate herself into *his* affections... It was really too much.

Her cheeks felt painfully hot as Justin pressed his cool, wet face against hers ecstatically. "Give it to you?" she repeated tightly.

"Yeah." Justin wriggled happily. "Taylor said the horse baby and me have to grow up a little bit, and then I can ride him all by myself."

"That's very nice of Melissa," she said, pushing the wet strands of fine dark hair out of Justin's eyes. She looked up, straight into Taylor's brooding gaze. "But I think she and Taylor should have asked Mommy about it first."

"We planned to," Taylor put in coldly. "But Mommy was busy protecting herself and she never came down to see us."

Justin had been in the operating room for two hours, the longest two hours of Brooke's life. She and Taylor sat side by side, but though he was so close she could feel the warmth of his arm through her sleeve, she couldn't remember ever feeling so alone.

Charlie, Mitch and Rose had all come, too—crowding the waiting room with their worried, drawn faces and effectively preventing Taylor and Brooke from speaking a single word in private. Which might, she thought, have been all for the good. She didn't know if her nerves could tolerate another argument with Taylor right now.

"I'm getting good vibes, I think," Mitch said halfheartedly, staring at the closed doors that led to the operating rooms. Brooke smiled a little, appreciating his motives, but Taylor didn't even seem to hear him. Charlie made a low, grunting sound, Rose patted the young man's arm once, and then everyone subsided again into silence.

Other families came and went, but their little group stayed as if frozen in their places. Another hour passed, and Brooke's head began to ache. The doctor had said three hours at most. Now every minute that went by could mean that something had gone wrong.

Three and a half hours into their ordeal, the outer doors opened. Brooke raised her eyes dully, not very interested. Just another worried father, an anxious mother, all keeping the same kind of harrowing vigil that she kept....

But it wasn't. It was Melissa, dressed in crisp white linen, looking as fresh and lovely as if she'd just stepped out of a magazine. She nodded a hello to everyone, but she hurried straight to Taylor and squatted at his feet, her hands on his knees, smiling up into his tired, sober face.

He put his hands over hers. "I told you not to come," he said, and then seemed to realize that wasn't the right reaction. "But it was good of you," he added with all the enthusiasm of a polite zombie. "I appreciate your concern."

The blonde's smile grew even more brilliant. "Oh, Taylor, I'm bringing more than my concern," she said, leaning even farther forward. "I'm bringing good news. The best news, I think."

She paused as if for effect. But Taylor's face didn't change. "What?" he asked in the same monotone, as though he couldn't imagine what could possibly matter right now. Brooke understood that sound—it was the echo of her own intensely concentrated inner fears.

"Charlie's office has been trying to reach him," Melissa said. "They finally called my house to see if I knew where the two of you were." She took a deep breath, signaling that she had come to the climax of her story. "Oh, Taylor," she said, her voice rising on a soaring note of elation. "They've found Kristina's brother."

Taylor's face didn't change, as if he had trouble understanding Melissa's words. "They did?"

He still sounded numb, Brooke thought. But she wasn't numb. She could already feel the fear blooming hot and cruel in her breast. She put her hands up against her chest as if she could hold it back.

"Yes," Melissa went on in her eager, strangely triumphant voice. "They've found Samuel. And he's confessed everything, Taylor. Everything you suspected was true—he forged your name to the documents because he had to push it through quickly."

"Why?" Brooke heard herself saying the word suddenly, unwilled. To her surprise, she was standing up. "Why would Samuel say that? He knew I wanted Justin. He knew I'd wait forever if I had to."

Melissa looked over at Brooke for the first time. Her gaze was cold, nothing like the supportive glow she had fixed on Taylor. "He says he was the one who couldn't wait," she replied in a clear, cool voice, enunciating every word carefully, as if she wanted everyone in the room to hear. "He says he needed the money."

Taylor's eyes sharpened, looking alive for the first time all evening. He focused that alert, razor gaze on Brooke. "What money?"

She felt the whole room listening, and she wondered, as if from a great distance, which of them—if any— would believe her story. It was like a noose tightening around her. Any wriggling she did would simply draw the rope tighter.

So she didn't squirm. She stated the fact with as much courage as she could muster. "I paid him ten thousand dollars," she said quietly.

She had expected an eruption of disbelief, of horror... but not a sound disturbed the unnatural quiet of the waiting room. It was as if no one had been able to believe their ears.

"Why?" Taylor's voice was flat, as though he already knew the answer. She knew how damning it must look to him—the rushed adoption, the forged signature, the payoff. "Why did you do it, Brooke?"

There was nothing to do but tell the truth. Whether he believed her or not, it *was* the truth, and she refused to be ashamed.

"Samuel always needed money," she said, pretending there was no one else in the room, focusing only on Taylor's green-gold eyes. "Jimmy and Kristina were always trying to help him out, though they didn't have much, either. After they died, Samuel told me he could get at least ten thousand dollars if he put Justin into a black-market adoption in his own country."

Melissa scoffed openly. "For a badly burned infant? I hardly think so!"

"Maybe he was lying," Brooke said, never taking her eyes from Taylor. This wasn't Melissa's business. "But I couldn't take the chance. He told me he had been in touch with you. That you'd already said you didn't want Justin. And, you see, I knew that you and Jimmy had been estranged for years, so I had no trouble believing that."

"No," Taylor agreed. "You've never had any trouble believing the worst of me."

She thought of Jimmy's angry diatribe against Taylor. Perhaps if Taylor knew the things his brother had said, he would understand why the story had seemed so plausible. But she couldn't tell him, not even to save herself. Jimmy had been too cruel, too full of drunken resentment. Taylor must never know that Jimmy had died with that much bitterness in his heart.

"At any rate, I did believe him," she said, refusing to be drawn into a fight. "I knew that if I left Justin with Samuel, he would end up in one of those hellholes they called orphanages."

She swallowed hard, thinking of the lost children housed like cattle. Taylor had probably never seen anything that terrible in his life—he probably couldn't even imagine the abject misery of it.

"Samuel would never have bothered to care for Justin himself. He had already informed the hospital that he wouldn't pay the expenses incurred immediately after the bombing. The bills quickly ate up what little Jimmy had left, and when that was gone, Justin was stuck into a charity ward.''

If only Taylor had been there—if only he had seen with his own eyes . . . He would know why her one clear thought had been to get Justin back to the U.S. as soon as he was well enough to be moved.

"So when Samuel told me I had to pay him ten thousand dollars or he'd call the adoption off, I agreed. I never hesitated for a moment. I never bothered to ask myself what a judge back home would think. Quite honestly, I didn't give a damn.''

Taylor stood completely still, so motionless that he might have been a painting of a man. His eyes were dark, fixed intently on Brooke's face.

"Now, of course, I can see how it must seem to you," she said, her voice sounding slightly unsteady for the first time. "But I swear to you, Taylor, I never believed for one minute that Samuel had done anything to rob you of your rights. I would have hated to lose Justin, but I would have been glad, so terribly glad, for his sake if you had wanted him.''

His hand twitched. "Perhaps that would be easier to believe," he said, his eyes harder than ever, "if you hadn't been so horrified when I finally did show up.''

"But surely you can understand how different that was," she said, anger seeping into her voice in spite of her determination to remain calm. "By then, Justin had been mine for almost two whole years. He wasn't just a helpless baby who needed protection. By then, he was my son.''

Taylor didn't understand, though—she could feel his resistance, his disapproval. His hard eyes hadn't flickered once, hadn't softened even the slightest bit. He opened his mouth, and she knew what must be coming—

But she never got to hear it. Another voice broke in.

"Mr. and Mrs. Pryce?" Dr. Portland was at the door, his mask pulled down around his chin. "You can come in now—Justin is awake." He smiled warmly at their blank expressions. "I'm glad you're still here. He's very sleepy, but he's already asking to see you. Both of you."

CHAPTER ELEVEN

THE masks they had to wear hid everything but their eyes, distorting facial expressions, concealing so much that Brooke had no idea what Taylor was really thinking, really feeling, as he walked into the recovery room and saw Justin lying there, so small among all the equipment, so helpless beside all the machines.

The little boy was drowsing again, obviously still under the lingering influence of the anesthetic. Brooke's eyes filled with tears when she looked down at him, so frighteningly tiny and piercingly sweet in sleep. There would be pain later—a lot. She'd been with him through enough of these grafts to know how difficult his recovery could be. The anesthetic was a short reprieve. For that, for him, she was grateful.

Silently, she took her place at one side of the bed, clinging with white knuckles to the railing as Taylor positioned himself at the other.

Neither of them had spoken a word to each other since the doctor's arrival. Dr. Portland had done most of the talking, explaining how well Justin had done, how optimistic he was for the survival of the graft.

He would give them ten minutes with Justin, he said, and then he wanted them to leave. Justin wouldn't be out of recovery for a couple of hours, and then he would be sedated all through the night. Taylor and Brooke, the doctor said pragmatically, might as well go home and get some sleep.

At that point, Taylor had spoken up, explaining that they preferred to sleep at the hospital if a room could be found for them. Portland had been reluctant, but

Taylor had been persuasive, and he had carried the argument easily. They would go home for some clothes, he said, and then they would come back and take turns watching over Justin.

Brooke had been surprised, but tremendously relieved. When she had suggested this before, Taylor had opposed it, labeling it more of Brooke's overprotective hovering. Perhaps, she thought, he had learned something today about the pain that could come with loving. Perhaps, after sitting in that waiting room, just yards away from Justin, but unable to help him, he would understand the fears that had been driving her for the past two difficult years.

Her heart heavy, she studied Taylor now, as he stood looking down at Justin. She recognized that position so well, that half-bent straining toward the child. How often had she stood just that way, willing her own strength into Justin's little body? How amazing, how wonderful, really, that now the little boy had two people standing guard....

But for how long? She wasn't a fool. She knew that Samuel's confession had forever poisoned her relationship with Taylor. There could be no more dreams of a real marriage, a real family. Her legal position was shakier than ever. She'd be lucky if she could persuade any judge to give her even partial custody of Justin.

She bit her lip behind the mask. She couldn't think about that now, or she would fall apart right here, where she most needed her strength. She had to concentrate on Justin tonight. Her own fears would have to wait until tomorrow.

Justin stirred, shifting his head on the pillow, mumbling something that Brooke couldn't quite understand. She tensed, listening, and felt an answering tension from the other side of the bed.

Finally, after what seemed an aeon, Justin opened his eyes. He looked from one to the other, bestowing on each of them a groggy smile.

"Hi, sweetheart," she whispered around the lump in her throat. Each time, after each operation, the moment he swam up out of the anesthetic was like a little miracle.

"Hi," Taylor said, his voice husky. "How're you doing, champ?"

And then it happened. With a muffled murmur, Justin reached out with his tiny, sleepy fingers. He reached, in his innocence, for the one whose touch he needed most.

He reached for Taylor.

Taylor shot Brooke a brief, inscrutable look over the edge of his mask, and then, barely missing a heartbeat, he put out his hand and touched Justin's fluttering fingers. "It's okay, champ," he said softly. "We're here."

Gripping the steel rail so hard her palms stung, Brooke stared at those two hands that fit so well, that were so perfectly entwined. She watched as the strong hand trembled, tightening protectively. And she watched when, just seconds later, the tiny fingers loosened, drooping slowly away. Justin, safe in his uncle's hands, had fallen back to sleep.

She choked back a sob, and she looked up just in time to see the odd glistening at the corners of Taylor's eyes. He didn't look up. He seemed completely unaware of her gaze, unaware indeed of the tears themselves. They welled, bright and silver, until finally they overflowed their banks, sliding slowly down his hard cheekbones and disappearing like smoke into the stiff blue fabric of his mask.

The drive back to Raven's Rest was pure torture. Rose, who had requested a ride home, tried to keep the conversation going, but neither Taylor nor Brooke helped much. The air in the car was miasmic, thick with unexpressed emotion.

Brooke hadn't wanted to leave the hospital at all, but Taylor had insisted, and his tone had left no room for argument. She knew, of course, why he wanted her to go with him. He had things to say to her, recriminations too ugly to be spoken in front of the others. Rose's presence in the car was all that held him back now, but Brooke knew the storm would break as soon as they were alone.

To her surprise, he went straight into his study when they arrived at the house. Calling the private detective? she wondered. Confirming Melissa's report before he let loose his fury? She went slowly upstairs to pack. He would come when he was ready.

It was difficult to enter the bedroom again. Another silver night had fallen, but this one was so different.... She dropped onto the edge of the bed, staring at herself in the mirror. She didn't sparkle tonight. She was gray, muted, as indefinably sad as fog or mist.

With a wretched, distant part of her mind, she wondered how, exactly, the details would be handled. Taylor would not want her to stay here. He might even expect her to go away willingly, chastened, leaving Justin behind.

But she wouldn't do it. She couldn't do it.

She didn't care what the whole world thought. She didn't even care what Taylor thought, not about this. She was not guilty. If he fought her, she'd appeal the custody case all the way to the Supreme Court. She'd take it to the Pearly Gates if she had to.

Somewhere, somehow, she would find a judge who understood that her only real sin had been one of gullibility. In her naïveté, she had believed that honest motives were their own defense. She hadn't bargained on having to prove anything as intangible as good intentions in a court of law.

She hadn't really expected to have to prove them here at home, either. Childishly, she had believed that her love for Taylor would be enough.

She clenched her fists in her pockets. Perhaps if they had been married longer... Perhaps if it had taken a few months for his detective to find Samuel... Maybe then, Taylor would have learned to care, learned to trust. But they had had only a few days, only one silver night.... It hadn't been enough to build on.

Her fists rustled against something in her pocket, and with effort she remembered that she had tucked Mitch's notes and brochure there. All the suggestions for next year's flower garden...

She fingered the crumpled papers with an unexpected flare of eagerness. She stood and, going to the door, flicked on the overhead light. She packed quickly, and then she hurried down the stairs. She left her overnight case beside the door and let herself out into the night.

The moon was on the wane, but it was still bright enough to illuminate the rose garden with its white stone benches and concrete fountains at each corner. Though she knew the roses bloomed in every color of the rainbow, tonight they all looked strangely silver in the moonlight.

She propped herself on one of the benches, and pulling out the brochure and one of Justin's colored pencils, she began to sketch a garden. Her imagination and her fingers flew. Canterbury bells over there, perhaps. Forget-me-nots on the other side...

Though she might well have to leave this house, she would leave something behind, something that would be alive and beautiful. Something that would last. A crazy idea, maybe—but it seemed to ease the ache around her heart.

Soon she heard footsteps, echoing crisply in the clean night air. She looked up from her sketches with reluctance. It was Taylor. She put her hand over the picture as if to protect it from his critical gaze. She wasn't quite finished.

"Brooke." He stood at the edge of the rose garden. "What are you doing out here?"

She held up the seed catalog. "Mitch asked me to help choose biennials for next year."

He cocked his head, and a moonbeam slid across the dark waves of his hair. "You're doing that now? Before we go back to the hospital?"

She looked away. "I thought I'd better."

There was a small silence, which she interpreted as disapproval. She gathered up her sketching things, hunting for Mitch's scribbled notes, which had fallen to the side.

"I've already packed," she said quickly. "I'm ready. But we aren't really terribly late. He'll be asleep for another hour at least—"

"Don't get up," Taylor broke in. "Mitch is bringing the car around in a few minutes. I want to talk to you before we go."

She subsided, unsurprised, and stared at the brightly colored brochure without seeing a thing. She had known, of course, that this was coming, and she had decided to let him speak his mind without protest.

But his first words were not at all the ones she had expected.

"I've always known that Jimmy hated me the last few years of his life," he said, ambling slowly into the garden, touching a rose here, a leaf there, as if it were just any normal stroll through his grounds at high noon. As if this were just any conversation.

Shocked, she made a slight sound of demurral, but he stopped her with one sharply raised hand.

"No, don't let's waste time," he said flatly. "You've been admirably restrained about repeating his comments, but believe me, it isn't necessary. Whatever he said to you about me—well, he probably said all that and more to my face."

Brooke was bewildered by this opening. "He was very bitter," she admitted. "Though he wasn't particularly specific. I never really understood what had happened."

Taylor laughed, a mirthless sound that carried on the dark air. "It all boiled down to money, I guess," he said. "Doesn't everything?"

How tired he sounded, she thought. He wandered to the bench that had been placed opposite hers and sat. They faced each other over a low birdbath that held the face of the moon in its wet black bowl.

"I'll have to start at the beginning, I guess. My father announced his plans to disinherit me when I was twenty." Taylor sounded slightly bored, as if this recitation of ancient history was no more than a necessary nuisance. "He wasn't a man to make idle threats. When he died a year later, he left everything he owned to Jimmy. The business, the money, this house..."

"But my God—why?" She couldn't hide her shock. What on earth could Taylor have done to deserve such a final, complete rejection?

"My parents went through an ugly divorce. My mother had been unfaithful, and my father was half-mad about it, I think. He told Jimmy and me that we were never to speak to her again." He shook his head. "I thought that was spiteful and grossly unfair to Jimmy and me— and, like a fool, I told him so. I went instantly, defiantly, to visit my mother, and when I came back I learned that I had been disinherited."

"Oh, no..." She hardly knew what to say. What a monster his father must have been!

He took a deep breath. "Yes," he said dryly. "At the time, it came as quite a shock. I was engaged, but I discovered pretty quickly that my fiancée didn't have much interest in a man with no expectations. She dropped me before the ink was dry on the new will and found herself irresistibly attracted to my brother.''

"Melissa," she breathed.

He nodded curtly. "You knew? Did Jimmy tell you that, too? It didn't last long, though in all fairness Melissa did seem genuinely in love with him. But he was definitely not ready to settle down."

She didn't say anything. Any of the usual phrases would have been clichéd, useless. No wonder Charlie had said that Taylor would never take Melissa back.

"Anyway, Jimmy wasn't ever very good with money. He had bad judgment, a gambling problem and very little impulse control. Within a few years, he had run through all his cash."

Brooke could believe that. She had seen Jimmy run through Kristina's money, too—at least until Kristina had put her foot down. Too bad there hadn't been a tough-minded lady like Kristina in his life much earlier.

"Much to Jimmy's annoyance, while he'd been blowing his fortune, I'd been out making mine. When he finally had to put Raven's Rest up for sale, I bought it. Mine was his only serious offer—he'd let it go to seed—and he was too desperate to turn me down. That's when he began to hate me, I think. He believed I had bought it just to spite him." Taylor turned his face to the moonlight and took a deep breath. "And he was right."

Brooke shook her head. "Oh, surely not. It was your childhood home."

He lowered his head, smiling grimly. "Sorry, Brooke. At the time, I didn't give a damn about that. I was mad as hell, and I did it just to spite him."

She could find no words of comfort, indescribably saddened by the note of self-recrimination she heard in his voice. Surely he had had reason to be angry. He had been horribly mistreated.

"That's when Jimmy left the country. I had no idea where he went. At first, I told myself I didn't care, but you can't kid yourself forever. After a year or so, I had become fairly frantic. I had a detective looking for him, but I was going at it all wrong. I told him to look in the decadent places—anywhere Jimmy could drink hard and gamble at someone else's expense." He shrugged. "Oddly, we never thought to look for a married man living modestly in a tiny little war-torn country in the middle of nowhere."

Brooke didn't speak, afraid to interrupt.

"Anyhow, I just wanted to tell him—" he paused "—that he could come home. I wanted to tell him that Raven's Rest was his if he wanted it, that I had fixed it up, that he could come on home, and we'd find a way..."

He brushed his hand through his hair. "You know the rest. By the time I traced him, he'd been dead for more than a year. The records over there were abysmal—everything had been burned down or blown up. Or maybe Samuel had deliberately tried to cover his tracks. Who knows? But the bottom line was that I didn't even know about Justin until I finally read some old letters that had been found among Jimmy's things. The letters mentioned a pregnancy."

He turned toward her, his face deeply shadowed. "After that, it took me another year to find out what had happened to Justin, but I never gave up. I had to bring him home. I couldn't give Raven's Rest to Jimmy, but I could give it to his son."

He shifted on the bench, took another deep breath. "Long way to the point, isn't it? But do you understand what I'm trying to tell you?"

"I'm not sure," she said carefully. "Are you trying to explain why it's so important that Justin live here at Raven's Rest with you? Because if you are, I ought to warn you that, however much I sympathize—"

"No," he cut in roughly. "Damn it, Brooke, I'm trying to explain that I believe you. I'm trying to tell you that I know I brought this on myself. If I hadn't been so eager to rub Jimmy's nose in his failures, he wouldn't ever have left the country. He certainly wouldn't have spoken of his brother as such a bastard. And you wouldn't have been so ready to believe that I was the kind of man who could turn his back on his orphaned nephew."

She stood up, her legs hot with a rush of adrenaline. "I know I *did* believe that, Taylor. But I didn't know you. I didn't know how wrong Jimmy was—"

"He wasn't wrong," he said. "I *had* been a bastard. My father was to blame for disinheriting me—not Jimmy. Melissa was to blame for being faithless—not Jimmy. But I took my anger out on him instead. He had every reason to hate me."

"Taylor..." She stood there uncertainly. She wanted to go to him, but she wasn't sure she would be welcome. It was hard to read this strange mood.

"And then, as if I hadn't learned a damned thing from what happened with Jimmy, I did the same thing to you."

"No—"

"Yes. Kristina's brother is the person who stole Justin from me, not you. If anything, you saved him. And yet I blamed you, even dared to resent you for the intimacy you shared with him. I even wanted to take him away from you, if I could." He turned toward her, his face strangely harsh. "I'm sorry for all of that. I know those are just the same stupid words people use to apologize for burning the toast...but I don't know what else to say." His jaw pulsed. "I'm just so damned sorry if I hurt you."

With one desperate move, she broke past the dam of her uncertainty—she crossed the little garden and went to him, sat beside him on the cold stone bench.

"Don't get your hopes up, Brooke." He looked at her with eyes that glittered strangely. "I know this is where I'm supposed to be noble, to tell you that I relinquish my claim on Justin—and my claim on you, too. But I can't. No matter how guilty I feel for forcing you into this sham of a marriage, I won't let him go." He narrowed his eyes. "I won't let *you* go."

"Won't let *me* go?" Her heart began to pump frantically. "But—if you don't want to get rid of me, if you weren't looking for evidence to invalidate the adoption, why have you been searching for Samuel?"

He frowned. "Because I had to prove I didn't abandon my nephew, of course."

"Prove it to whom? To a court?"

"No." He put his hands on her shoulders roughly. "To you, damn it. To you."

She couldn't speak. She stared at him, confused.

"From the very beginning, you threw that accusation up at me. I hadn't wanted to be tied down, you said. I hadn't wanted a damaged infant to interfere with my wicked life, my women and—well, God knows what all Jimmy told you."

His voice was deep and hard. "I couldn't stand seeing it in your eyes every time I tried to touch Justin, every time I tried to talk to him. And I damn sure couldn't stand seeing it in your eyes every time I tried to kiss you."

He looked at her lips, and they tingled, remembering. "I knew there was no hope for us, not unless I could prove to you that someone else had signed my name to those godforsaken papers."

She latched on to the three words that seemed somehow to stand out from all the others. "Hope for us?" She felt slightly dazed, and she knew she must sound absurd, following his logic so slowly, so fearful of misreading him. "What do you mean? You persuaded me to marry you. We became lovers. What more were you hoping for?''

He hesitated before answering, as if he was measuring his words carefully. ''I was hoping,'' he said finally, ''that you would learn to love me.'' She drew in a sharp breath, and his fingers tightened on her shoulders. ''I think I fell in love with you the first moment I saw you. I knew I was going to have to make you mine any way I could.''

She wondered if she might be dreaming. It didn't seem possible that he had really said these things. These miraculous, marvelous things...

''But when I agreed to the marriage, you seemed so...cold,'' she said. ''I was afraid you regretted having asked me.''

''I almost did.'' He smiled ruefully. ''I wanted more. You accepted me out of fear, under the threat of losing your son. I wanted you to come to me out of love, driven to say yes by the same kind of crazy need that was tormenting me.''

''I was,'' she whispered as her body began to tremble. ''I do.''

''Do what?'' His gaze locked with hers as if he could pull the admission out of her.

''Do love you,'' she said, drowning in his eyes. ''Do want you. Do come to you tormented by a need I can't control.'' She took a ragged breath. ''I think I had learned to love you before I ever even met you. You and Justin are so much alike, you know. When I saw you that first night, I had such a strange, wonderful sense of knowing you, of belonging with you. I've always thought that was why I let you take me home—because I saw Justin in your eyes....''

He lifted a hand to cup her cheek, and as his warm palm touched the wetness there, she realized that she was crying.

"I'm disappointed," he said, his voice husky. "I thought you were a victim of my amazing sexual allure."

"Well, perhaps it was just a little of that, too." She smiled through her tears. "But it's been so long." She put her hand on his chest. His heart pounded against her palm, and the rhythm was like a long lost dream. "I may need a refresher course...."

He laughed; the sound was music. He put his hand over hers. "I'm sorry, Mrs. Pryce. We've reserved a hospital bed for tonight, as I recall. I'm afraid all classes in amazing sexual allure will have to be postponed."

"Hmmm." She ran her hand across the stiff cotton of his shirt. "Well, all right. Maybe we should spend the evening making a few adjustments in our prenuptial agreement anyway."

"Such as?"

"Such as the party of the first part is not allowed to spend more than fifteen minutes alone with Ms. Melissa Duke."

He chuckled. Turning her around, he gathered her up against him so that her head was cradled against his shoulder. "Done. Provided you're forbidden to associate with Clarke Westover."

Reaching up, she touched his throat and felt the pulse leap under her fingertip. "Gosh, that's a tough one," she said, her voice rippling with laughter. "No Clarke at all? Who will pick out our champagne?"

He kissed the top of her head. "No Clarke, no Charlie, no Mitch. They're all a little bit in love with you, you know. Especially Mitch." He made a low noise in his throat. "I'll tell you right now—if that young jackass doesn't stop ogling your aura, he's going to be pushing up roses, not planting them."

She wriggled against him, amazed that a simple admission of jealousy could be so delightful. So endearing. So downright sexy.

"Okay, I guess." She sighed. "But we'll have to pencil it in as one of your duties to keep my chakras balanced and my aura rosy." She tilted her head to look once more into his beautiful green-gold eyes. "Every day. Till death us do part."

She heard the sound of the car pulling up in the driveway, ready to take them back to Justin. He smiled down at her, burying his lips in her hair.

"It will be my pleasure, Mrs. Pryce."

Let's Celebrate!

LOVE & LAUGHTER™

invites you to
the party of the season!

Grab your popcorn and be prepared to laugh as we celebrate with **LOVE & LAUGHTER**.

Harlequin's newest series is going Hollywood!

Let us make you laugh with three months of terrific books, authors and romance, plus a chance to win a FREE 15-copy video collection of the best romantic comedies ever made.

For more details look in the back pages of any Love & Laughter title, from July to September, at your favorite retail outlet.

Don't forget the popcorn!

Available wherever
Harlequin books are sold.

 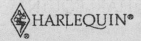 

HE SAID

SHE SAID

Explore the mystery of male/female communication in this extraordinary new book from two of your favorite Harlequin authors.

Jasmine Cresswell and Margaret St. George bring you the exciting story of two romantic adversaries—each from their own point of view!

DEV'S STORY. CATHY'S STORY.
As he sees it. As she sees it.
Both sides of the story!

The heat is definitely on, and these two can't stay out of the kitchen!

Don't miss HE SAID, SHE SAID.
Available in July wherever Harlequin books are sold.

HARLEQUIN®

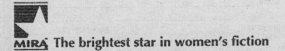